ADAM'S IMAGE

*Recent Titles by Debbie Macomber
from Severn House*

COUNTRY BRIDE
A MARRIAGE OF INCONVENIENCE

ADAM'S IMAGE

Debbie Macomber

This first world hardcover edition published 2016
in Great Britain and in the USA by
SEVERN HOUSE PUBLISHERS LTD of
19 Cedar Road, Sutton, Surrey, England, SM2 5DA,
by arrangement with Harlequin Books S.A.
First published 1985 in the USA in mass market format only.

Map by Ray Lundgren.

British Library Cataloguing in Publication Data

Macomber, Debbie author.
  Adam's image.
  1. Man-woman relationships--Fiction. 2. Love stories.
  I. Title
  813.6-dc23

ISBN-13: 978-0-7278-8597-5   (cased)

All Severn House titles are printed on acid-free paper.

Severn House Publishers support the Forest Stewardship Council™ [FSC™],
the leading international forest certification organization.
All our titles that are printed

MIX
Paper from
responsible sources
FSC   FSC® C013056
www.fsc.org

Printed and bound in Great
TJ International, Padstow, C

For Mr. and Mrs. Stephen Kersten.
Many happy years, many happy children.

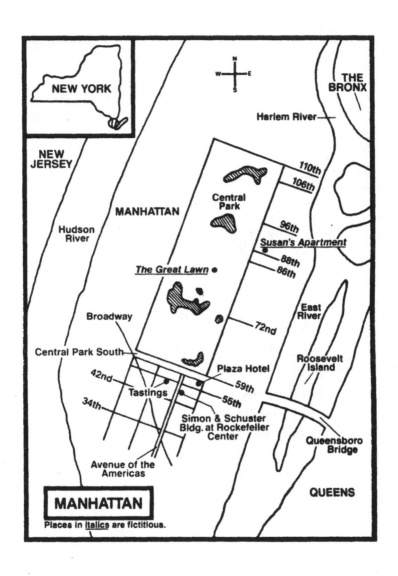

Chapter One

He stood across the room, nursing his drink. Not for the first time that evening, Susan Mackenzie found her attention drawn to the tall, rather lanky man. Her first impression was that he was strikingly unattractive. His face was too narrow, the chin square and abrupt; the dark brown eyes were friendly, but small. And his hair, although short and well trimmed, did little to disguise ears that tended to stick out. But there was a kindness about him, a gentleness she hadn't seen in a man for a long while.

Susan was situated in a corner by herself. Cocktail parties were not her forte. She tended to be more comfortable communicating with an individual instead of a whole room full of strangers. But she had seen to the obligatory chitchat and was free to sit and observe.

Several editors from rival publishing houses were present and Susan enjoyed looking them over, learning what she could about the people from the way they interacted with others. The games they played—the games everyone played—could be amusing when viewed from a spectator's position.

That was what interested Susan about the stranger across the room. He too was an onlooker. Twice she had watched couples approach him. His smile had been warm and genuine, and although Susan couldn't hear his voice over the conversational hum, the sound of his laugh had drifted across the extensive living room, deep, rich and full. Just listening to him had made her want to smile. He gave whomever he was speaking to his full attention. A man who listened, another rarity.

She stood, taking her wineglass with her as she approached him. He saw her coming and straightened slightly. Susan wondered if he'd noticed her and shared some of the same thoughts.

·"Susan Mackenzie." She held out her hand.

"Adam Gallagher." He took her petite hand in his huge one and shook it firmly.

"I wanted . . ."

"I was going . . ."

They both spoke simultaneously and stopped to laugh.

"You first," Adam said, and gestured with his old-fashioned glass, his dark eyes smiling.

"I don't believe we've met, and thought I should take the opportunity to introduce myself." There were probably dozens of people she hadn't met tonight, but he was the only one who interested her enough to seek out.

"I was thinking the same thing."

"Are you a friend of Ralph's?" Ralph was the man giving the party. The cocktails were part of the celebration for Ralph, who was opening his own literary agency after several years of working for L & L Literary Services.

"We attended college together." He smiled, displaying a flash of pearl white teeth. "Are you in publishing?"

Susan nodded. "Associate editor." She could feel his surprise although he didn't comment. People were often amazed that someone as young as she would be an editor. It wasn't uncommon; most romance editors were in their mid to late twenties. Nearly everyone at Silhouette's office was. Susan was twenty-four. "And you?"

"No." He shook his head. "I'm a doctor."

Now it was her turn to be surprised, although why she should she didn't know. The profession fit perfectly with the man, his kindness, the gentle quality about him. He was a healer.

"Do you have a complaint?" he asked with a rueful gleam.

"A complaint?" The questioning look produced small dimples in her naturally rosy cheeks.

"You know, headaches, a bad back, indigestion?"

A breathless laugh came from her as he held her gaze. "Now that you mention it," she said, "my feet are killing me."

"New shoes?"

A strand of long brown hair fell loosely down the side of her cheek as she nodded. Susan looped it around her ear.

"Would you like to sit down?" he suggested.

What she wanted was to go home, but not if it meant missing the opportunity to talk to this intriguing male. There were quite a few things she planned on finding out about Adam. She liked him, had liked him almost from the first moment she'd begun observing him. That in itself was unusual. "I suppose I should."

Adam left momentarily and returned with two chairs. "Here, that should take some of the pressure off your feet."

They sat and talked for an hour. Adam told her how he'd met Ralph and how they'd maintained their friendship over the years. Susan's own dealings with Ralph Jordan had been limited. Most of his clients wrote mainstream fiction, although he represented one of Silhouette's best authors. That was why she was there tonight.

Adam wasn't shy, and somehow she found that surprising. He wasn't like her; he didn't possess the same reasons for blending into the background that she did. Her reticence came from a deep-seated shyness that she had struggled to overcome most of her life.

The more they talked, the more attractive Adam became. Less than an hour after she introduced herself, Susan no longer saw the too square chin, or the large ears; she saw the man. And the man was the most compelling, interesting one she had met in two years of living in New York.

Adam paused and glanced at his watch. Something flickered over his face. "My goodness, I've been talking up a blue streak." A scowl briefly touched his brow. "I don't usually do that." He stood. "Would you like a refill?" His gaze centered on the empty goblet she held in her hand.

"No, I'm fine. Thanks."

He examined his own empty glass. "What I'd really like is a cup of coffee. How about you?"

"I doubt that we'll find that around here." Had she unconsciously hoped he'd suggest they go someplace else?

"Sure we will, come on." His hand cupped her elbow as he directed her toward the back of the house. His touch was gentle, assuring, pleasant. While they'd been talking she had studied his hands. They were exceptional. Large, with long tapered fingers and square-cut nails. If she had noticed them before they spoke, she might well have guessed he was a doctor.

"Hey, Adam, who's the pretty girl?" A husky male voice impeded their progress.

Susan felt Adam tense. He dropped his hand from her elbow and let it fall to his side. Although he gave no outward sign, Susan could sense that Adam didn't like the man behind the voice.

"Susan, this is Tony Dutton." The introduction was made grudgingly.

Nodding politely, she purposely didn't offer Tony her hand. He was one of the men she had studied earlier, flittering from one beautiful woman to another dispensing his male charm like a bee collecting nectar from a variety of flowers. Sleek, handsome, a womanizer.

It hadn't taken her more than a minute to recognize his type.

"Tony."

"Hello, Susan." He drawled her name as he did an appreciative sweep of her appearance. His gaze paused on her full breasts and then her soft mouth. "Just where have you been all night?"

"With Adam." She hoped to convey her lack of interest in the clipped reply.

"If you'll excuse us," Adam inserted, his hand again gripping the underside of her elbow.

Tony looked taken aback for a moment, but he quickly recovered and gave Adam a bold wink. "Sure thing, good buddy, sure thing."

Again Adam gave no outward sign, but Susan knew he was repulsed. He directed her through the small groups that were milling around chatting. He stopped at the entrance to the kitchen and held open the swinging mahogany door.

"Betsy will make us a cup of coffee."

A large-busted woman of about fifty was preparing a tray of hors d'oeuvres. She turned at the sound of someone intruding on her territory, the blue eyes stormy. But the minute she recognized Adam, the frown turned to a wide grin.

"Dr. Gallagher," she exclaimed in delight. The high-pitched voice was filled with devotion. "I wondered if you'd come back to see ol' Betsy."

"I couldn't very well leave without saying hello to my favorite girl, could I?" he joked, giving the older woman a bear hug.

"Oh, be away with you." Betsy laughed, and a

dancing gleam sprang from the tired face. "I suppose you're after a piece of my apple pie again."

"Not this time," Adam said, and moved slowly to Susan's side. He reached out and took her hand; the touch, although impersonal, produced a warmth within her. She was beginning to feel some of the things her writers spun stories about.

"Susan and I would like a cup of that marvelous coffee you brew."

Hand on her hip, Betsy glared at him mockingly. "Excellent brewed coffee, indeed," she quipped. "Been serving the same brand around this house for ten years. Nothing fancy, either," she mumbled under her breath as she brought down two mugs from the cupboard. "Comes straight from a can."

With a boyish grin creasing the grooves at the sides of his mouth, Adam pulled out a kitchen chair for Susan.

"I'll take care of that, Betsy."

"Sit down," the gray-haired woman ordered. "I won't have anyone fiddling in my kitchen but me."

Adam's gaze met Susan's, and the quirk of his thick brows showed his amusement.

No more than a minute passed and they were served mugs of steaming coffee and thick slices of apple pie with hot cinnamon sauce. Susan wasn't hungry, but she wouldn't have offended the older woman. The pie was delicious.

Adam carried their plates to the sink when they'd finished, and kissed Betsy on the cheek. Susan watched as the woman flushed with pleasure. Lifting the glass coffee pot, he brought it to the table and refilled their cups.

Susan leaned back in the chair and held the mug with both hands.

"Here." Adam sat beside her and lifted her feet onto his knees. "If you take these off, you'll be able to relax. Nothing can ruin an evening more than shoes that are too tight." Carefully he unbuckled the strap and slipped the sandal off her foot, letting it drop to the floor. Gently his fingers massaged the toes, the circular motion extending to the arch of her foot. The gentle rotating action was repeated on the other foot.

The ache all but disappeared as a tingling sensation ran up the back of her legs. Susan felt her throat tightening as she struggled not to purr. The sensations he was producing in her were incredible. The featherlight touch was strangely, inexplicably intimate. She lowered her lashes because to look at him would reveal the havoc his touch was playing on her senses.

"Are you asleep?" The question was whispered.

"If I am, I don't want to wake up," she answered in a subdued, husky voice.

"Me either." The words were issued so quietly that Susan wasn't sure he'd spoken.

She opened her eyes to watch his gaze move slowly over her.

"You're very beautiful." He'd stopped massaging her feet. "Those eyes are fantastic. I don't think I've seen anything so brown in my life."

From any other man it would have sounded like a line designed for its devastating effect. But not from Adam.

"Your hair is the same warm shade as your eyes. I imagine I'm not the first man who's wanted to run his fingers through it."

Their gazes met and held, and for an unbelievable moment Susan felt as if she'd never need to take another breath. Again she was forced to restrain herself. It took every dictate of her will to keep from standing and pulling the combs from her hair to allow the long chocolate brown curtain to fall free. Her heart was pounding so loud she was sure he must hear it. His gaze lowered to rest on her generous mouth. He didn't need to voice his thoughts; they were there for her to read.

A dish clanged against the counter in the background, breaking the spell. Adam shifted uneasily and looked away. "Want some more coffee?"

Susan shook her head because speaking would have been impossible.

"I'll buckle these for you." Leaning over, he gripped the straps of one black leather sandal and slipped it onto her foot.

"You make me feel like Cinderella." Susan had attempted to make a joke, but her voice sounded incredibly weak.

"I'm no Prince Charming." The cynical tone of his voice surprised her.

A frown of confusion knit her brow. "Is something wrong?"

He paused, compressing his mouth into a thin line. "No. I'm sorry."

"Adam." Her hand reached out, and her fingertips

gently stroked the angular line of his jaw. "Would you kiss me?"

He caught his breath audibly, his eyes burning into hers. "Now? Here?"

A smile tugged at her mouth as she nodded in answer to both questions.

His eyes turned a deeper shade of brown as he stood, looking around him.

Susan's gaze followed his. Betsy was busy at the kitchen sink, her back to them. At the moment Susan wouldn't have cared if they'd been in the middle of the living room with its tens of guests; all she knew was that she didn't want to wait another minute to discover what it would be like to taste his mouth once it was placed over hers.

"Outside." An arm around her waist led her out the back door. A dim light illuminated the cement patio. At least, Susan thought it was a light; maybe it was the moon.

There wasn't much time to survey their surroundings before Adam slipped his arms around her and brought her against the muscular hardness of his chest. His hold tightened and his mouth moved closer.

Susan linked her arms around his neck and stood on tiptoe, anticipating the union of their mouths. Adam didn't rush the process. His eyes seemed to burn into hers. The tip of her tongue moistened suddenly dry lips, and with a muted groan, Adam lowered his mouth to hers.

The kiss was soft and gentle, as if she were as delicate and precious as fine porcelain. Parting her lips in welcome, Susan yielded. A rush of intense pleasure washed over her and left her trembling. The kiss deepened as his hands roamed over her back, arching her closer and closer as if he wanted to fuse them together for eternity.

When Adam dragged his mouth from hers and buried it against the side of her neck, Susan felt cheated. This shouldn't end; it was too beautiful, too right. She was on the brink of discovering in a few short minutes more of what it meant to be a woman than she had in all her twenty-four years.

She was conscious of the pressure of his body pressing against her and of Adam's uneven breaths. Had he felt it too? Surely he must have . . . certainly he knew.

She gave a small protesting moan as he pulled away. His hands moved to her upper arms as he took in deep, ragged breaths.

"You are very kissable," he murmured, his eyes half-closed. "But then, I imagine more than one man has told you that."

Several had, but Susan didn't want to think about anyone or anything except Adam. How could she possibly hope to explain that she felt more wonderful with him than she had with any man . . . ever. Was it conceivable that she could be falling in love with someone she had met that night and had kissed only once? Even to herself it sounded ludicrous.

Placing two fingers over Adam's lips, she hoped to silence him. "Your mouth is equally desirable." Leaning forward slightly, she softly pressed her lips over his.

His hands tightened as if to restrain her, but the tenseness quickly flowed from him. Instead of pushing her away as she was sure he intended, he gathered her to him, holding her in his embrace. One palm rested over his heart and Susan sighed as she felt the erratic hammering beat. The flame that was blazing within her had touched him too. She couldn't remember a time she felt more happy, more content.

"Susan." Her name had become a gentle caress as he held her, his chin resting on the crown of her head.

She breathed in deeply, drinking in the scent of musk and cinnamon.

"We should be getting back," he said, and she could feel his mouth move against her hair. The reluctance in his voice made her want to sing.

"We've probably been missed by now."

"Probably," Adam said with a sigh.

But neither moved, unwilling to break their embrace. Just knowing that he was sharing these same inexplicable feelings excited her almost as much as being in his arms.

"Are you cold?" Adam questioned as if suddenly conscious that the early-October night might be uncomfortable on her bare shoulders. His hands ran up and down the silky length of her arms in an effort to chase away any chill.

Susan couldn't prevent the small laugh. "Cold? Are you joking?"

"I guess that was a silly question." Adam spoke softly.

Silence stretched between them. The party would be breaking up soon, and although he continued to physically hold her, Susan could sense him mentally withdrawing. The horrible sensation that they would part tonight and she would never see him again tightened the muscles of her abdomen. The thought, even after this short a time, was intolerable. Yet Adam said nothing, made no suggestion they meet.

"Can I see you again?" She asked with an eagerness she didn't often reveal. "Tomorrow?" she asked with a half smile.

"I'm on duty at the hospital in the afternoon." He drew away, dark eyes narrowed on her face.

"Morning's fine. I'm an early riser." Normally she was anything but. It wasn't often that she could think clearly without a minimum of two cups of strong coffee.

"I've got a soccer game."

"You play soccer?" He'd be a natural. Tall, lean, quick. For a moment the image of Adam running down a field, manipulating the ball with agile feet flashed through her mind.

"I coach a team for the Boys' Club." He drew in a deep breath. "Not tomorrow, maybe sometime next week. I'll give you a call." The softness had left his face.

Stunned for a moment, Susan stared at him disbelievingly. His mood had changed so quickly. "You're giving me the brush-off, aren't you?" She had come on strong, a lot stronger than she did with others. Some men didn't like that. Adam was obviously one of them.

"I'm not." Just the way he said it told her he was lying.

Susan took a step in retreat, studying him in the soft moonlight. She clenched her hands nervously. A chill that had nothing to do with the weather raised tiny bumps over her forearms. For the first time she saw displeasure in Adam's features. His jaw was clenched and tight; a muscle twitched by the corner of his eye.

"Don't worry, I get the message. Don't call me; I'll call you." She laughed tightly. Pride dictated that she hold her head high; her chin was tilted at a slight angle. "I've got better things to do than wait around for a phone call."

"I'm sure you do." The words sounded grim, final. "I enjoyed meeting you, Susan. I wish you well."

"Oh, me too," she replied flippantly. "It's been grand, just grand." With a sweeping gesture Loretta Young would have envied, Susan turned. "Now if you'll excuse me."

"Of course."

The back door closed and Susan thought it must have weighed three thousand pounds. It felt so heavy and hard. But then, so did her heart. Pausing just inside the kitchen, she glanced out the window. Adam remained exactly as she'd left him, a solitary figure standing in the moonlight. His shoulders had hunched, and she watched as he wiped a weary hand over his face. Indecision and some kind of inner turmoil seemed to be troubling him.

"Mighty fine man." A voice sliced into Susan's thoughts, and she swiveled her attention around.

"Pardon?"

Betsy was wiping her hands on a linen dish towel. "I said Dr. Gallagher is a fine man."

"I'm sure he is." Susan meant that sincerely.

"Not much to look at though." The older woman

chuckled, but her eyes were serious as they seemed to appraise Susan. "That means a lot to some people. My Ben was a good-looker. Biggest mistake of my life was marrying that man. Caused me nothing but heartache all his life."

"Looks aren't everything," Susan agreed, walking across the kitchen. "Thanks for the coffee and pie, Betsy."

The woman's gaze followed her. "Good night, miss."

"Good night." The words nearly stuck in her throat.

"Did you have a good time last night?" A sleepy, disheveled Rosemary Thomas sauntered into the cozy living room and looked questioningly at Susan early the next morning. Rosemary was employed in Silhouette's contract department, and the two shared a tiny one-bedroom apartment off east Eighty-eighth Street.

"As good as can be expected." Susan sat sideways on the sofa, burrowing her feet beneath the opposite cushion as she sipped from a steaming mug of coffee. The dark liquid burned her lips, and she blew into the cup before taking another drink. The coffee was bitter.

"Meet anyone?" Rosemary persisted while pouring herself a cup. Long auburn hair tumbled over her flannel nightgown.

The dark eyes widened. "What makes you say that?"

Rosemary shrugged one delicate shoulder. "I don't know, you look different. Brooding, like you ate too much pâté or met Mr. Wonderful."

"I didn't eat the pâté, and I've given up on the dream of ever finding Mr. Wonderful."

"Do my ears deceive me?" Rosemary placed a hand dramatically over her heart. "How can a romance editor forsake Mr. Wonderful?"

"Mr. Wonderful's an illusion," Susan announced, turning her head to avoid looking at her friend. "I'm looking for Mr. Nice Guy."

Rosemary sat in the worn chair covered in the same material as the sofa. She lifted her knees and pulled the long nightgown down over her legs.

"What did you do with your hair?" Susan asked, noticing for the first time the way the auburn curls seemed to spring in every direction. "You look like you stuck your finger in a light socket."

Rosemary giggled good-naturedly. "I gave myself a perm last night. I think I may have left the solution on a bit longer than necessary."

A smile threatened to crack the tight line of Susan's mouth. "You may have."

"Doing anything this weekend?" Rosemary asked, taking her first sip of coffee. She paused to grimace. "What'd you make this with? Shoe polish?"

"No to both," Susan answered evenly.

"I think I'll head out after breakfast. It's Mom's birthday Wednesday, and she'll be disappointed if I don't spend some time with her. You're welcome to come if you want."

With a quick shake of her head, Susan declined the invitation to visit her friend's family in New Jersey. Her hair flowed unrestrained down her back and seemed to dance with the movement. "I've got some proposals I want to go over this weekend." Bringing work home from the office was essential in order to keep current with the demanding load. Working with as many as fifty authors made it impossible to find the time to read all the material she wanted and give it her undivided attention. Therein lay the root of the problem. Constant interruptions were all part of being an editor.

The remainder of the weekend passed in a dull shade of gray. With Rosemary gone, Susan spent the rest of Saturday and all day Sunday going over material from the slush pile. Some of the best authors Silhouette published had started out by submitting unsolicited material. One of the most fulfilling aspects of her job was the chance to spot and develop new writing talent.

Wednesday afternoon, Susan did something that shocked her. She phoned the Boys' Club and discovered the youth soccer games were played at nine and ten-thirty on Saturday mornings in Central Park.

If she felt like a fool then, she felt more of an idiot the next Saturday as she zipped up a baby blue warm-up jacket and headed for the park.

"Why am I doing this?" she repeatedly asked herself as she walked the distance. Brilliant fall colors cloaked the avenue as multicolored trees lined the entrance. The day was glorious. One of the few remaining Indian summer days that would grace New York, Susan thought. At least it wasn't pouring rain. If she planned on running into Adam, she had to make it look as if she were on a casual stroll enjoying the weather.

The soccer fields were on one end of the Great Lawn, exactly where the man at the Boys' Club had said they would be. A quick glance at her watch, and Susan noted it was ten to nine. She hadn't been up before nine on a Saturday morning in six months; Rosemary would be shocked to wake and find her gone.

The playing fields were chalk lined. She didn't know that much about soccer, except what she'd read the night before in the encyclopedia. It seemed to be a natural sport for young children and didn't require much finesse or skill. Only the ability to run and kick.

As she advanced toward the fields, Susan picked out Adam easily. He stood head and shoulders above—and in several cases was a couple of feet taller than—the nine- or ten-year-old boys on the team.

Just watching him, even from this distance, did something to her heart. What was it about this man that had haunted her all week? She couldn't sleep without dreaming of Adam. And if the nights were bad, the days were worse. There hadn't been a single day that she didn't force herself to rein in her thoughts or force Adam's image from her mind. What had happened that night at Ralph Jordan's for him to suddenly pull back, withdraw from her? In the beginning she was sure it was because she'd come on so strong. Some men preferred shy, retiring females. But there had been nothing that evening to indicate that those were his views. After all, she had been the one to make the first move and introduce herself. That had seemed to please him. She had even asked him to kiss her. Color invaded her face at the memory, creeping up from her neck. Even then he had shown no displeasure. Everything had seemed to indicate that he was as caught up in this attraction as she.

This whole thing was probably an occupational hazard for her, something that came as the result of reading thousands of romances. Leaning back against a huge oak tree with one foot propped against the bark, Susan expelled her breath slowly. That's not what it was and she knew it. She had been attracted to Adam Gallagher physically, mentally and spiritually almost from the moment she'd first seen him.

The players were on the field, and at the sound of the official's whistle one player ran forward and the ball was kicked. Knobby-kneed boys raced from one end to the other with boundless energy. Even from her position, camouflaged by the trees, Susan discovered she couldn't remain unaffected. Several times she kicked her own foot as if the movement would aid the players. When Adam's team scored the first goal, Susan all but leaped in the air with excitement.

On more than one occasion Adam cupped his mouth to shout instructions to his team. She might have been out of earshot, but it was easy to see these boys adored him.

Sometimes—Susan didn't know why—the action was stopped and a boy would step onto one of the sidelines and throw the soccer ball onto the field. Immediately a fierce scramble would result and the game would resume.

The official's whistle blew, and for a moment Susan thought the game had ended. Instead the players ran off the field and Adam's boys huddled around him. Adam knelt on one knee in front of the group.

Half time, she mused. The second half of the game proved to be as exciting as the first. Adam's team won the game, and Susan couldn't restrain her sense of pride. Her intention had been to saunter past him casually and act shocked that they happened to run into one another.

Now she realized she couldn't do it. Turning, she stuck her hands in her pockets and headed toward the sidewalk, her feet kicking up the leaves as she walked.

Ten-fifteen and the park was alive. She took a deep breath of the autumn air.

"Susan." Someone was shouting her name.

She turned to see Adam running toward her with long strides. He was slightly breathless when he caught up with her.

If she'd hoped for a friendly greeting, she was in for a disappointment. His eyes were dark and brooding. Forbidding.

"What are you doing here?"

Chapter Two

"Oh, hi. Adam, isn't it?" Susan hoped to give an impression of indifference.

But the knowing look his eyes flashed at her told her she hadn't fooled him. Yet she persisted in the charade.

"I just happened to be enjoying a walk and stumbled onto the soccer game. You have a good team. Nice day, isn't it?"

"Beautiful." Adam smiled ruefully.

"Well, I won't keep you. I've got some errands to do," she said with forced cheerfulness. "It was good seeing you again. Give Ralph my best." She offered him a weak smile and turned. *He's actually going to let me leave,* her mind screamed. *He's going to let me walk away without saying a word!* She kicked at the leaves with the toe of her shoe, angry with him and the world.

27

She didn't need to turn around to realize he was standing there watching her. His eyes seemed to be boring holes into her shoulder blades.

Without even knowing she would do anything so crazy, Susan collapsed to the ground. Totally relaxed, she slumped onto a huge mound of leaves the parks department had collected.

"Susan."

Never had she heard so much emotion in the simple sound of her name.

The clamor of running footsteps followed. At precisely the right moment, she turned and threw a huge handful of maple leaves into his face.

Adam looked stunned, his hands fighting off the attack of foliage. Before he could recover, she stood, picked up another armload and tossed those at him.

Susan was laughing harder than she could remember doing in a long time.

Adam stared back at her in bewilderment. "What did you do that for?"

"Because I couldn't stand for us to talk to one another like polite strangers," she yelled. "What's the matter, don't you like to fight?" Bending down, she scooped up more leaves, preparing to do battle.

She never got the chance. One gentle push against her hip toppled her onto the soft pile. Immediately she was deluged with leaves as Adam dumped several armloads over her head.

In an effort to escape, she rolled onto her side, kicking up the leaves as she turned. Laughter hindered her movement, and a second later Adam had joined her on the ground, his hands pinning her to the earth.

Her breasts heaving with the effort to breathe evenly, she gazed into the powerful face that had haunted
her all week. Amusement glittered from his dark eyes,
and the corners of his mouth were quivering. Their
looks met, and the world about them seemed to fade
into oblivion. The leaves, the sun, the trees were gone,
as were the sounds that filled the heart of Central Park
in New York City. The hold on her hand relaxed, and
Adam brushed the hair from the side of her face. His
touch was gentle, sweet. The laughter had left his face
as his attention centered on her softly parted lips.

Susan inhaled deeply, anticipating the union of their
mouths. He didn't want to kiss her; she could see it in
the determined set of his jaw. But at the same time, he
couldn't stop himself. The knowledge thrilled her, and
instinctively her arms curved around his back as he
lowered his head.

The kiss renewed every sensation she had experi-
enced the night they met. Somehow deep inside she'd
been hoping it had been the wine or the romantic
surroundings. The memory of being held in his arms
and standing in the moonlight filled her thoughts. But
she was kidding herself. This was real, so real and
wonderful. Magic.

She hadn't realized she'd whispered the word until
Adam raised his head, his look quizzical. "Magic?" he
repeated.

She smiled and nodded, her hand fitted over his
cheek; the growth of day-old beard gently prickled the
skin of her palm.

Adam released her and sat up. He linked his hands
around bent knees and stared into the distance.

Susan joined him, sitting in the same position. "Why?" she murmured softly. There wasn't any need to explain the question. The one word asked so much. Why had he made it plain he didn't want to see her again after the party? Why had he looked so unwelcoming when she'd come to the park? And why was he so reluctant to kiss her?

"I knew someone like you once," he began, and there was a deep sadness in his voice. Still he didn't turn to look at her. "Gail was as beautiful as you are."

"Pretty girls are a dime a dozen." She shrugged her shoulders and looped a long strand of hair around her ear. The movement captured Adam's attention.

"She had the most incredibly thick auburn hair."

Susan hated her already. "Mine's brown." Expelling her breath forcefully, she rested her chin on top of one knee.

Adam didn't seem to notice her; he was entangled in his own thoughts. So he'd been hurt, she thought, probably jilted; maybe his red-haired beauty was dead. None of it had anything to do with her. Unless . . . unless he had been pretending he was holding Gail, kissing Gail.

"Are you still in love with her?" she questioned bluntly, desperately needing to know.

Adam looked taken aback for a moment. "I don't think so. No." He shook his head, adding emphasis to the response.

"Well, that's encouraging." She didn't mean to sound ill-mannered, but love's course hadn't been all that smooth for her either. She didn't know that it was for anyone.

She bounded to her feet, suddenly angry. The one thing she thoroughly detested was being confused with someone else, especially when that someone else happened to be his one true love. "It was nice seeing you again, Adam. As always, it was an adventure."

He stood too, brushing the leaves from his pants. He started to say something but she interrupted him.

"The name's Susan, in case you forget. That's S-U-S-A-N. It doesn't even come close to Gail. And the hair's brown, dark brown." She weaved her fingers through its length. "And for that matter, I'm not all that beautiful. My nose is a little odd. But you hold on to the illusion of Ms. Perfect. I'd hate to be the one to force you to come to terms with reality." Pivoting sharply, she strode with purpose-filled steps out of the park. He didn't try to stop her. Somehow she knew he wouldn't.

Susan lifted her eyeglasses and pinched the corners of her eyes with her thumb and index finger. This job was definitely taking its toll on her eyes. She coughed. Her health too. The little romp in the damp leaves last Saturday had resulted in a horrible cold. That's what she got for behaving like an idiot. A sneeze was coming, and Susan grabbed a tissue just before the gigantic burst of air shook her body.

Another violent sneeze caught Rosemary's attention that night. "You know what you need, don't you?"

If Susan heard about the wonders of vitamin C one more time she thought she'd scream. Her roommate had been on a health-food kick for weeks. For her own part, Susan felt she ate a balanced diet, half good food and half junk food. "I can't imagine what, Dr. Pauling."

Rosemary had the good grace to look slightly abashed. "Well, yes, vitamin C would help, but what would really help is some good old-fashioned exercise."

"That's how I got into this mess in the first place, if you recall."

Rosemary shook her head. The perm had been tamed considerably and was styled attractively, feathered away from the petite oval face.

"I'm serious," her friend said forcefully. "What you need is to get those endorphins pumping through your body."

Susan sighed and shook her head scornfully. "Endorphins? Have you been reading too many Intimate Moments again?"

"I can't believe anyone can graduate from Cornell and not know what endorphins are."

Susan sneezed again. Her throat ached and her eyes were beginning to water. She couldn't miss any work; her desk was stacked high enough as it was. She looked at Rosemary, who was bright and cheerful while she felt wretched. "All right, tell me all about it." She might as well capitulate. From the look in her eye, Rosemary would tell her anyway. Why fight it?

"Endorphins are a secretion your body produces that gives you a natural high, both physical and mental. I was reading about it in one of the books I picked up from the health-food store. The book said that exercising will actually make you feel good. That's why I've started to walk to work."

For over a month Rosemary had trekked the two and

Scratching her head, Rosemary quirked her mouth to one side. "I don't know. Let me check the book again. Keep your head down until I get back."

"Wonderful, just wonderful," Susan muttered, feeling wretched. "This had better work, Rosemary. And if you dare say a word to anyone . . ."

"I wouldn't, don't worry." Mockingly, she crossed her heart. "Now keep your head down."

Obediently, Susan replaced the towel and sat in a dejected heap on the edge of the bathtub, breathing in the citrus-scented steam.

Somewhere in the distance she heard a buzzer. It sounded as if it had come from the stove in the kitchen. Susan groaned inwardly, wondering what other wild concoctions Rosemary assumed she could get away with. As it was, she'd about had it.

"Susan, it's for you."

Her fingers gripping the edge of the towel, she lifted her head and peered out. "What's for me?"

"The door."

"The door?" she repeated, dumbfounded, and as she did her heart leaped wildly to her throat. Adam Gallagher moved into her line of vision, standing directly behind Rosemary.

"Hello, Susan. It's Adam, spelled A-D-A-M."

Immediately Susan lowered her head, hiding under the towel. "Rosemary," she shouted, "do something."

"I didn't know he was following me," Rosemary defended her actions. "I thought he'd sit down." Apparently her friend found it necessary to exonerate herself.

"I should have," Adam said, a smile evident in his

voice. "But I confess to being curious about a certain smell that seemed to be coming from this room."

"Would you two mind leaving?" Susan screamed, and seethed silently. Nothing in the world could induce her to remove the towel. She would prefer to sit and evaporate in the steam than have Adam see her like this.

At the sound of the door closing, Susan ripped the garlic from her throat and let the towel fall to the floor.

Dear heaven, she'd never be able to look Adam in the eye again. How would she ever live this down? Both hands covered her face as she sat in misery.

A couple of minutes later there was a light tap on the door. Without waiting for a response, Rosemary stuck in her head.

The thin line of each delicately shaped brow was arched in question. "You're not mad, are you?"

Susan gestured weakly with one hand. "Why should I be? Just because I was made to look like a complete idiot? Just look at me, Rosemary." She held up two limp strands of wet hair, and her voice wobbled. "How could you do this to me?"

"I'm sorry, Susan. Really sorry."

Dismissing the apology with a wave of her hand, Susan turned toward the bathtub. "I'm going to do what I should have done in the first place. Take a hot bath, down two aspirin and go to bed. And if there's a merciful God in heaven, I'll die peacefully in my sleep and never have to face the world again."

As much as Susan hated to admit it, she felt much better the next morning. Rosemary had already left for work, but there was a note waiting for Susan beside the coffee pot on the kitchen counter. It read: "Hope you feel better. Adam wanted me to ask if you'd meet him tonight, six o'clock at Tastings for a drink. I would have said something last night, but I didn't think you were in the frame of mind to talk to me. I don't blame you. Hope to see you later. Rosie."

Her frame of mind last night had been strictly forbidding. After a long soak in a hot bath, Susan had gone directly to bed. Rosemary had watched her anxiously as Susan walked from the bathroom to the bedroom. But the tight set of Susan's mouth had apparently convinced Rosemary to leave well enough alone.

Susan picked up the piece of paper, crumpled it and tossed it into the garbage can. Every encounter she'd had with Dr. Adam Gallagher had been disastrous. Why make a fool of herself again? She wouldn't go.

By the time she broke for lunch that afternoon, Susan had decided she was behaving childishly. Of course she'd meet Adam. Wasn't that why she'd gone to Central Park Saturday morning?

Sure, she countered mentally, but that was before she knew about his long-lost love and how much she reminded him of Gail. Her mind spat out the name distastefully.

At five-thirty, Susan cleared her desk, or as much of it as she could. There seemed to be a sense of never really being finished. There were always more manuscripts, more correspondence, more stories. If she didn't love the work and New York, her job could have depressed her. Instead she was challenged.

No, she wouldn't meet him. What was the use? She wouldn't be a stand-in for any woman.

Making polite conversation in the elevator with her co-workers, Susan wasn't sure what she was saying or even to whom she was speaking. Her thoughts were muddled. Her heart was telling her she should meet Adam. But the more practical part of her personality was issuing repeated warnings that pursuing a relationship with him would eventually lead to pain and heartache.

Without ever admitting to herself she would or wouldn't accept the invitation, Susan strolled toward Tastings, a popular restaurant six blocks up the street from the Simon and Schuster Building. She preferred to think that she was leaving her options open. At any time she could turn around and head for the apartment.

Early October and the day was glorious. The air was crisp, and she stuffed her hands into the long beige raincoat. Her heels clicked against the cement walk as she strode purposefully along her way.

Adam was arriving just as she got there. Maybe if Susan hadn't seen him, hadn't felt the physical stirrings just looking at him created in her, maybe then she wouldn't have kept the appointment. But she did see him. He was there, walking toward her with a wide grin that was directed at her alone. And like a magnet drawn to steel, she returned his warm greeting with a smile of her own.

"Hello, Susan."

"Adam." She couldn't look away. He really was plain looking. He was tall but muscular, and his wide shoulders narrowed to lean hips and long, long legs. Plain, but compelling in a way she couldn't describe.

"I see you're feeling better," he said with a smile. "Your roommate mentioned you were under the weather."

Susan flushed, silently praying that he wouldn't say anything about last night. "Yes, much better. Thank you."

A low chuckle rumbled from his throat. "The wonders of modern medicine never cease to amaze me. I was rather shocked to discover such advancements since I left medical school."

"Adam Gallagher." Susan stopped midstep. "If you so much as mention one word about last night, I'll leave."

A large hand cupped her elbow as a mesmerizing smile crinkled the lines at the corner of his eyes. "No more, I promise."

Tastings was a long and narrow room with emerald green tablecloths on the square tables. One wall contained a huge wood bar with upholstered stools. Behind the bar was a glass case containing the hundreds of bottles of expensive wines Tastings was known for. It was a popular place to meet for drinks. Although it was early evening, the room was nearly filled. Adam found an empty table and helped her out of her coat. He folded it along with his own over the back of a chair. A waitress took their order and returned a couple of minutes later with Susan's California Cabernet Sauvignon and Adam's French Beaujolais Nouveau.

Adam cupped the long-stemmed glass, and again

Susan was impressed with his hands. A smile briefly touched her mouth as she thought there was a magical quality about his fingers. She had known doctors before, had even dated one briefly a couple of years ago. But no one had affected her the way Adam did.

His shoulders were hunched forward slightly, and Susan asked, "Tired?"

He ran a hand over his eyes and nodded. "But it's not the company I keep." His gaze rose to meet hers. "The stork got me out of bed this morning about four. A beautiful baby girl, but the mother had a difficult labor and I wanted to be with her. Her husband left her, and she was alone and needed someone. By the time I finished there, it was time to go to the office."

It's not his hands, Susan mused, but his heart. His capacity to love and care was larger than any man's she had known. He was the kind of person who would carry the whole world on his shoulders if it would help someone.

"We can make it another time if you'd rather," Susan offered.

"No." He reached across the table and squeezed her fingers. "In fact, I don't know about you, but I'm starved. I'm not dressed for anything fancy, but I know where we could find a decent meal."

Susan nodded, pleased at the invitation. "Yes, I'd like that."

He took her to a small restaurant not far from Times Square that served charcoal-broiled hamburgers and fresh-baked bread. The owner shook hands with Adam and personally escorted them to a booth. From the way the man spoke, it was obvious that he'd been a patient.

Adam introduced Susan, and Ambrose Lockridge shook her hand so hard Susan was sure she'd lose feeling in her fingers.

Ambrose wouldn't allow them to order from the menu, insisting he would personally cook the specialty of the house in their honor.

"You'll have to forgive him." Adam looked faintly chagrined. "Ambrose tends to be overenthusiastic."

"I don't mind," Susan insisted, her face gleaming with an inner happiness. Some men would have felt the need to impress her with an extravagant restaurant, but not Adam. In his own way, he was making a statement about himself. He preferred the simple life.

Their seats were situated against the outside wall by a window that ran the length of the building. Susan watched, fascinated, as dusk settled over the most exciting city in the world.

Ambrose delivered hamburgers that looked as tall as the Empire State Building. Melted cheese, sliced pickles, thick slices of tomato, lettuce and a sauce oozed from the sides of the buns. The meat patty alone must have weighed half a pound. One person couldn't possibly manage to eat the entire hamburger.

Susan did her best, downing almost half. Again she discovered how much she liked Adam. He talked for a long time, telling her about his office and the decision to go into family practice, which in itself was a specialty. He told her a little about the woman whose baby he had delivered that morning.

Not until they finished their meal and several cups of rich coffee did he mention Saturday morning. "I feel I owe you an explanation."

Taking a sip from her coffee cup, Susan avoided looking at him. She didn't want to hear about Gail; she wanted to build her own relationship with him. Leave the past buried.

"You don't owe me anything, Adam," she said, hoping to conceal the frustration in her voice. "I got the picture from what you said Saturday."

"I'm sure you thought exactly the wrong thing," he contradicted gently. "I wasn't comparing you to Gail, although there are striking similarities."

"I doubt that very much." Susan took another sip of coffee. The hot liquid felt good against the slight thickening building in her throat.

"I like you, Susan."

He was saying so much more. Susan wished she knew exactly what. Could the attraction he felt for her be half as potent as what she was feeling? She set the cup back on top of the table. "I like you too."

Again his gaze settled on her facial features. "You're a beautiful woman, and I'm not exactly a knight in shining armor."

"I'm not Lady Diana, either," she countered. If it would have made any difference, Susan would have gladly erased the smooth, silky skin, the brilliant brown eyes and gentle curves of her womanhood. With any other man her attractiveness would have been an asset. But not with Adam.

"You're prettier than royalty. Prettier than Gail."

Susan felt as if her heart would burst. She turned her troubled brown eyes toward him. "Did this . . . other woman hurt you so bad that you can't trust again?" Susan chose not to say her name.

"Gail," he supplied again, as his index finger did a lazy circle around the rim of the cup. "I loved her very much. But I was young and stupid."

Adam may love Gail, Susan thought, but she had never felt such intense dislike for someone in her life.

"Here," he said, and took the paper napkin from her hand. "If you don't stop, you'll have that thing shredded to a thousand pieces."

Susan wasn't aware that she had been doing anything to the napkin. "What happened?" she asked. Adam wanted to tell her; maybe it would help him finally obliterate Gail from his memory. Susan, however, wasn't so sure she could sit and listen while he spoke of another woman he had loved so intensely.

Adam's look was thoughtful. "We met when I was in med school."

That long ago! Susan thought with a sense of frustration. Adam had to be thirty-four, maybe thirty-five. He had loved Gail all these years? Involuntarily, she stiffened.

"There's really not much to say except that we fell in love. I fell in love," he corrected. "Gail fell for dollar signs she was sure were in my future. I should have known a beautiful, popular girl like Gail couldn't really love someone like me."

Susan had to swallow back words so as not to interrupt him. It had been on the tip of her tongue to say she was half in love with him and they'd only been together three times. Her declaration would have embarrassed them both.

"At the end of my first year we got engaged. A couple of months later my father became seriously ill and I decided to discontinue my studies and help out at home until Dad was better. Gail was adamantly opposed to my leaving school. We had a bitter argument. I couldn't understand how she could be so uncaring, so heartless toward my father. I must have been naive, because she chose to spell it out to me."

Undoubtably there was a lot Adam was leaving unsaid. "Anyway," Adam continued with brooding thoughtfulness, "I did go home, and my father died a couple of weeks later. I was glad I was there. By the time I returned to school, Gail was engaged to another medical student."

"And you still care about her?" The question was hurled at him in disbelief.

"No." His voice was a soft, caressing whisper. "But a man doesn't easily forget his first love."

They'd been lovers. The thought was so unbearable that Susan downed the remainder of her coffee in one giant swallow. What was the matter with her; was she going crazy? She had never been the overly jealous type. At least not until now.

"How can Gail and I possibly be alike?" she questioned grimly.

"In addition to being beautiful, you both have the tendency to go after what you want. Neither of you is easily dissuaded."

Pinching her lips tightly closed, Susan released an inward groan. She knew it! They had gotten off to a bad start because she'd been the one to cross the room and introduce herself. She'd asked him to kiss her, and when it looked as if he wasn't going to suggest they meet again, she'd said something. Not only that, but she had another mark against her because she'd gone to Central Park hoping to see him on Saturday. If Adam only knew how extraordinary such behavior was for her. Never, she promised herself, never again would she instigate anything with him.

"I'm not like her, Adam. But that's something you'll have to discover yourself." She straightened and reached for her purse.

For a moment he didn't reply. "I was afraid you thought I was pretending you were Gail when I kissed you. I wasn't." His voice was husky and soft.

Susan doubted he raised his voice to anyone. He was a gentle man. Scooting out from the chair, she stood and reached for her raincoat. "I should be going. Thanks for the drink and dinner," she murmured.

Adam stood and paused to place some money on the table before taking his coat and following her outside. She heard him call something to Ambrose.

The sky was a magnificent purple and pink. Silhouetted against the skyline were huge buildings of concrete and steel. But she hardly noticed.

A hand on her shoulder halted her progress as she moved to the street to wave down a taxi. "Just a minute." Adam expelled his breath forcefully. "I've offended you, haven't I? That wasn't my intention."

Susan already knew that. Adam would never knowingly hurt anyone. "I'm sure it wasn't," she replied stiffly, keeping her face averted so she could capture a cab's attention.

"When you're in my arms, Susan, I can think of little else."

Well, she certainly hoped so! With one foot off the

curb, she looked down the street. Where were the taxis when she needed one?

"It doesn't matter to me if I'm at a party with tens of guests, any one of which could step onto the patio. It doesn't matter that it's the middle of Central Park on a bright fall morning." The pressure of his hands turned her around. His eyes were smiling into hers with a mischievous light. Slowly he lowered his mouth to claim hers in a gentle but surprisingly ardent kiss.

Susan melted into his arms as he wrapped her in his embrace and half-lifted her from the sidewalk. A soft, involuntary moan came when he lifted his head, but he quickly lowered it again, parting her lips with a plundering kiss that sent the world in a tailspin. Obviously one kiss wasn't enough for him, either.

Susan buried her face in his light jacket and sighed unevenly. Adam's mouth was pressed against the top of her head. "What should it matter if I kiss you in midtown Manhattan?" It wasn't really a question.

A taxi pulled to the curb. "You looking for a ride?" he asked in a surly tone.

"Yes," Adam answered for her.

With a determined effort, she dropped her arms. Adam held open the car door.

"Good night, Susan."

She smiled softly and pressed her fingers to her lips and waved a good-bye. Still caught in the rapture, speaking would have been difficult.

"Where to, lady?"

Susan had to stop a minute before relaying her address.

Not until she was almost home did Susan realize Adam had done it again. No mention had been made of seeing her again. And after what he'd said tonight, she couldn't invent opportunities to see him. For all she knew, Dr. Adam Gallagher was out of her life.

Chapter Three

Susan offered Jack Persico an apologetic smile. The bored, frustrated look he shot back didn't encourage her. The evening had been a waste. What was the matter with her? Couldn't she have fun anymore? Why should her life hinge on whether she heard from Adam Gallagher again? She hadn't, and that was the crux of the problem. For over two weeks she'd lived and breathed anticipation. As each hour, each day passed, she grew more uncertain.

"I had a nice time. Thanks, Jack," she murmured flatly, unable to force any enthusiasm into her voice.

"Little liar," he said, and laughed lightly. "What's wrong? Problems at the office?"

Shaking her head, she turned and inserted her key into the lock of her apartment door. "I hope you aren't offended if I don't invite you in, but I really am tired."

"I understand," he told her gently, and in a strange way Susan was sure he did. He gave her a knowing smile and kissed her lightly. One finger trailed a path across her cheek. "I'll give you a call later."

Her throat muscles constricted painfully. "Thanks, Jack." She let herself into the silent apartment. Rosemary had gone out after all, she mused. Leaning heavily against the door, she felt the hopelessness of the situation wash over her. Friday night and she'd turned down two invitations, hoping to hear from Adam. When she didn't, she accepted Jack's casual offer for a movie. A half hour afterward and she couldn't remember the title, let alone the plot. The entire evening had been spent worrying if she was missing a phone call. Maybe Adam had stopped by? Jack and several others were anxious for her company. Why was it the one man that mattered couldn't have cared less? Releasing a slow, uneven breath, she hung up her coat.

Just as she closed the closet door, Rosemary came out of the bathroom, her face covered with a green conglomeration that resembled avocados and mayonnaise.

"Oh, you're back. How was the movie?"

"Great. Any phone calls?"

"One, he didn't leave his name."

Susan's heartbeat nearly tripped over itself. Adam! "Was there a message?"

"No, he said he'd call back later."

Glancing at her wristwatch, Susan asked, "When did he call?"

"About an hour ago," Rosemary mumbled, barely

moving her lips as the facial plaster began to slip. "But I don't think it was your doctor friend. This guy sounded sexy."

"Adam's sexy," she shot back heatedly. Her dark eyes flared with defiance.

Rosemary looked stunned for a minute. "I know, what I meant was that this guy's voice was different from Adam's."

"Oh," she whispered, deflated. "What's that on your face?" Maybe if she changed the subject she could gloss over the small outburst.

"Avocados." The timer buzzed, and Rosemary returned to the bathroom.

Susan could hear the faucet running as she glanced over the *TV Guide* looking for a late, late show to distract her. Nothing but old monster films. Sighing, she tossed the guide on the end table and absently reached for a magazine. Two weeks! Why hadn't Adam called? He couldn't help but know how crazy she was about him. How could he not know? She'd practically thrown herself at him. If she'd given a dozen men half the encouragement she had him, they'd be married by now. Married. The word had slipped into her mind so easily. Almost from the beginning she'd recognized that Adam was what she'd been searching for in a husband. That gentle, caring quality about him made him so attractive to her.

The clock radio went off early the next morning and Rosemary groaned in protest. "Susan," she mumbled. "It's Saturday. Turn the radio off."

Stretching out a hand, Susan fumbled with the switch

that killed the music. One eye fluttered open to note the time—seven fifty-five. She hadn't been kidding herself; the alarm had been purposely set. Perhaps that had been Adam phoning last night. Then it'd be entirely proper for her to contact him in return. And since she'd been thinking about how good an early-morning walk in Central Park would be for her health, there was no better time than Saturday morning. If she just happened to run into Adam coaching his soccer team, then that would be the perfect time to ask.

Slipping out of bed, she grabbed jeans and a sweater and silently walked into the bathroom. With luck she could be out the door before Rosemary knew she was gone. Since she was unable to fool herself, she wasn't likely to outsmart Rosemary. In addition, she didn't feel like answering questions this early in the morning. As far as this health-food kick went, most of which Susan thought of as silly, she did agree with Rosemary on the importance of eight hours sleep. Something she rarely got, especially when they sat up to 3:00 A.M. playing Monopoly. And people thought editors lived glamorous lives.

Forty-five minutes later, fortified with several cups of strong coffee, Susan let herself out the apartment door. A chill ran up her arms as the crisp October air hit her face. One look at the threatening dark sky and she cringed. Only for Adam; there wasn't another reason on earth she'd be out this early on a Saturday morning.

Her breath formed a foggy curtain as brisk strides carried her into the park. After the initial chill, she had quickly become accustomed to the cold. Even walking had been pleasant. Maybe Rosemary wasn't so loony after all, and a little exercise was just the thing she needed. No, quickly she dismissed the thought. No need to be hasty.

After a few minutes of following the meandering cement walkway into the park's interior, she saw Adam. Pausing, hands clenched tightly in her pockets, she stopped and watched him for several moments. Her gaze was drawn to the craggy features, the proud look. It was unfair that after two miserable weeks she should be this affected by him. One glance and she felt relief flood through her.

Standing on the sidelines of the soccer field, Adam was talking to his team. Everyone clapped their hands once and ran onto the field. Even Adam. Dressed in jeans and a gray sweatshirt, he stood in front of the boys, who were in an orderly line. Even from the distance she could hear his shouts as he called and counted the exercises. First they did jumping jacks. Adam's arms flew into the air in perfect rhythm with his boys. Blood pounded in her veins at the virile sight he made. Pride touched her heart at the way the boys respected him. Much the same as she did.

Hoping to look as casual as possible, she strolled to the field and stood on the sideline. Her toe played with the chalk line that bordered the field. When she glanced up, her eyes met Adam's. She knew hers were round and a little apprehensive, but her doubts quickly faded at the welcome in his.

He shouted something to one of the boys, who ran forward and took his place. Agilely he trotted from the field to her side.

"Hi."

"Morning." She glanced away, fearing he'd read the eagerness she felt.

"I was hoping you'd come."

He was hoping she'd come! Her mind tossed back the words bitterly. For two miserable weeks she'd heard nothing from him. She'd turned down dates, sat by her phone, toyed with a hundred crazy excuses to see him, and he said he was hoping she'd come! Of their own volition, her eyes shot him an angry glare.

Surprise flickered briefly over his face. "Is something wrong?"

"Nothing," she lied. "I got a phone call last night. Rosemary said she thought it might have been you."

"No," he said casually, "it wasn't me."

No need to fool herself; she'd known it hadn't been. Inhaling deeply, she hoped to calm herself and fight off the attack of indignation. "It seemed like such a nice morning for a walk. I didn't mean to intrude."

"You're not," he assured her quickly, and exhaled a slow breath. "Are you always this beautiful in the morning?"

Beautiful! She'd barely worn any makeup, just a light application of lip gloss. Her hair was brushed away from her face and held in place with two barrettes. A hurried glance in the mirror on her way out the door had assured her that he wouldn't think she was planning to meet anyone.

Struggling for a witty reply, she murmured, "You should see me before I've downed two cups of coffee."

"I'd like that very much."

The words were issued so softly that Susan wasn't sure he'd said anything. But the way her heart somersaulted into her throat assured her she hadn't imagined it. When she turned to search his face, she found that his gaze was directed onto the field.

"We're going to need lots of encouragement today. We're playing the first-place team."

"Terrific," she said, and beamed him a smile. "I'll have you know I was a high-school cheerleader."

"It doesn't surprise me," he returned. "I suppose your school team went to the state championship."

"No." A puzzled frown marred her brow. "Why?"

"If I'd been on that team, I'd have played my heart out for you."

"You're on my team now, coach. So let's win this game."

Chuckling, Adam ran back onto the field.

As before, Susan was quickly caught up in the action of the game as the young boys ran back and forth kicking the black and white ball. Several calls made by the officials confused her, but rather than break Adam's concentration by quizzing him, she said nothing. But anytime Adam's boys had the ball, she gave her full support by shouting. As soon as she heard one of the boys' names, she called encouragements to him. The game was clearly a defensive one, and neither team had scored by half time.

The boys hurried and got a drink from the water faucet before gathering around Adam. Down on one knee, Adam drew a couple of pictures in the dirt with a stick, illustrating a play. Each youth was held in rapt attention. Adam asked a couple of questions, to which the boys nodded. A few minutes later the team was back on the field.

Like an anxious parent, Adam moved up and down the sidelines. Susan was convinced he'd forgotten she was there until one boy weaved the ball through the defenders and kicked it past the goalie, scoring for the first time. Before she knew what was happening, Adam's arms shot around her waist and she was lifted from the ground and swung around. Happiness gleamed from his eyes, and it was all Susan could do not to throw her arms around his neck and kiss him.

His team didn't score again, much to Susan's disappointment. Soccer could easily become her favorite sport if Adam took her in his arms every time his team made a point.

The final score was one to nothing, and the boys left the field triumphantly waving their hands high above their heads and shouting their glee. Again Adam gathered them around him. His eyes spoke of his pride as he congratulated each one. Every boy placed a hand in the center of the circle with Adam and shouted a cheer. They raced excitedly across the field to shake hands with the opposing team members. Adam stayed a couple of minutes longer to speak with the other coach, then turned and ran back.

The team had already gathered their coats and snapped up cookies and cups of hot chocolate one of the mothers was handing out.

"Congratulations, coach," Susan said with a warm smile when Adam joined her.

"I told you what would happen with you cheering," he said with a happy laugh. A hand on her shoulder brought her close to his side. "Have you had anything to eat? I'm starved."

"Me too."

"What would you like? The sky's the limit."

"Anything I like?" she asked, her voice low and seductive. "For openers," she said, and she swung her body around so that she stood directly in front of him. Placing a hand on both sides of his waist, she tipped her head back to look him in the eye. "For openers," she repeated, "I'd like to know why you haven't called me. Following an acceptable excuse, I want you to find a reasonably secluded corner and kiss me before I do something rash. And lastly, I'd like the assurance another two weeks aren't going to pass before I'm forced into making an excuse to see you." Taking in a deep breath, she continued. "And that's just the beginning."

Something unreadable flickered in his eyes, and his mouth thinned into an uncompromising hard line. Susan groaned inwardly, knowing that she had displeased him. She'd done it again. When would she stop making a fool of herself? Fiery color stained her cheeks. Adam preferred to handle their relationship in his own way, without her prodding.

Dropping her gaze and her hands, she stepped aside. "On second thought, a hot dog with mustard would do."

"But not for me," he murmured thickly. Fingers pressing the back of her waist, he directed her to a small stand of trees. Before she could say anything, he turned her into his arms. With his hands looped easily around her trim waist, his eyes, serious and dark, met hers. As if in slow motion, he lowered his mouth to hers. An eternity passed before his lips found hers in a kiss that told her everything she needed to know. He claimed her with a mastery that was unquestionable, as if he were a starved man invited to a banquet. His hands moved against her back, arching her closer, half-lifting her from the lawn.

As she linked her arms around his neck, her breath became ragged and irregular. One kiss and her senses were inflamed. "Two weeks," she moaned in frustration. "Why did you make me wait that long?"

"I don't know," he whispered against her hair. His fingers cupped her face and raised her head as his mouth crashed down a second time. The fierceness, the intensity stole her breath, and her knees threatened to buckle.

"Now for that hot dog," he whispered, and brushed his chin and jaw across the creamy smoothness of her cheek. His warm breath stirred the hair at her temple.

"Hot dog?" she repeated, still caught in the rapture.

"Food," he reminded her. "You said you were hungry."

"Oh, that." She tried to laugh, but the sound came out high and wavering.

He kissed her neck once fleetingly. The nibble shot delicious shivers down her back. "There's a place not far from here we can walk to if you don't mind."

"I don't," she assured him. Not when he had his arm around her; not when his eyes were laughing into hers; not when she felt as if she were walking on air.

As they strolled out of the park they met a vendor with a red cart selling giant pretzels. "Want one?" Adam asked. "They come with mustard," he added, as if she needed an inducement.

"Sure."

He handed the burly man some money and was presented with two doughy pretzels with mustard. Susan bit into hers and was surprised that they were still warm.

"Hey, these are good."

"You mean you've never had one of these?"

"To be honest, I've lived in New York two years and you wouldn't believe the things I haven't done."

"Climbed the stairs up the Statue of Liberty?"

"Nope."

"Visited the World Trade Center?"

"Nope."

"Toured the United Nations?"

"Nope."

"My goodness." Adam looked surprised. A hand cupped her elbow as they crossed the street.

"Visited the Museum of Natural History."

"That I've done, twice. I liked it so well the first time that I went back again." They continued strolling down Fifth Avenue with no clear destination. "There's one thing I've wanted to do. I mean, we don't have these things in Oregon."

"What?" He threw her a curious gaze.

"Subways."

"You mean to say you've lived in New York two years and you have never taken the subway?"

"Don't look so shocked. You're talking to a girl born and raised in Tillamook, Oregon. I thought I'd hit the big time at Ithaca."

"You attended Cornell?"

"Why are you so surprised? I'm not an air head."

"I know that." He took her hand and squeezed it tight. "Come on, I've got a gun permit. You'll be perfectly safe."

An entrance to the underground station was three blocks east. Adam paid for their tokens while Susan stared at the green walls littered with graffiti. Most everything was spray painted, and the messages scribbled across the walls were enough to curl her hair. "What's this, the library?"

Adam chuckled. "In a way you could say that."

"Well for heaven's sake, if they're going to write on the walls, the least they can do is learn how to spell. Some of their efforts are pretty creative."

Capturing her hand, Adam carried her fingers to his mouth, his eyes smiling into hers. "Do you find yourself doing this often?"

"Doing what?"

"Editing the world."

"All the time," she admitted. "I can hardly read anymore without changing a word here or there, or questioning punctuation."

The tender look he gave her created a whole series of new sensations within her.

"By the way, where are you taking me?" she asked as a way of disguising the overwhelming effect his touch had on her emotions.

"Wait and see."

A roaring sound filled the tunnel as the huge metal monster soared into view. Susan took an unconscious step closer to Adam. The roar dissipated into a swishing hiss and came to a stop. Steel doors glided open and several people filed out. Susan and Adam waited until there was a clear path before hurrying inside. The compartment was crowded with people from various walks of life. Businessmen, shoppers, and a few rough-looking souls who would have made Susan uncomfortable if Adam hadn't been standing protectively at her side. Because there wasn't any seating available, they stood. Susan kept her balance by clasping a steel pole. Adam's arm was wrapped around her waist to cushion her from any abrupt moves. At the first stop, the force of the train made her falter, and she would have stumbled backward if not for Adam.

"You okay?"

"Fine." Her voice was slightly choked, but not from the sudden movement. Adam had never held her this close for so long, and she couldn't help but marvel at the power he had over her senses. Everything about the day held a glorious promise, and she felt as if she'd been sipping champagne at noon instead of nibbling pretzels with a boys' soccer coach.

"We get off here," he told her as the train came to a halt a second time. Weaving their way between the other passengers, who weren't inclined to clear a path, they stepped off the train without difficulty. Adam's hand held on to her with a firm grip.

"What did you think?" he asked once they reached the street.

Tilting her head to one side, Susan shrugged. "I'm not sure. I do know I'm going to appreciate those surly cabdrivers a little more the next time I need to get someplace."

They'd walked several blocks before she ventured to

ask the question a second time. "Are you going to tell me where we're going or not?"

"You'll see."

Adam directed her into a multistory building on the next block, and he gave her an amused glance as he led her into the elevator and pushed the button indicating the tenth floor.

She ventured a guess. "Your apartment?"

Dark eyes feigned shock. "We hardly know one another."

"Adam," she groaned softly, "I hate surprises."

"I'll have to remember that at Christmas time."

The suggestion that she would continue to be part of his life pleased her more than she cared to reveal.

Stepping off the elevator, he took her hand again, not giving her the opportunity to study her surroundings. Together they walked down a long, narrow hallway. It didn't take her long to guess.

"Your office?"

"The girl's a marvel," he issued softly. His mouth curved into a tantalizing smile. "There's someone I want you to meet. But before I go to the hospital I've got to change clothes, and here is closer than my apartment. You don't mind waiting?" Thick brows arched with the question.

"Of course not, but, Adam . . ." She hesitated, glancing down at her jeans and leather loafers. "I'm not really dressed to be meeting people."

"No one's going to look past that gorgeous face to notice."

"Adam," she sighed in protest.

"You look fine, trust me."

"The last time someone asked me to trust them I ended up with garlic dangling from my neck."

Placing a hand on both shoulders, he brought her close. "I don't make many promises, but that's one I have no qualms about." He kissed her lightly, effectively silencing any further protest.

He brought her into his private office, then left to change in an examination room. Her gaze swept the walls, and she paused to read the framed degrees and certificates. Of more interest was a bulletin board in the reception room. She'd noticed it on her way in and was eager to examine it. Moving from his office to the front reception area, she saw pictures of newborn babies he'd delivered and several thank-you notes from children. A proud smile softly curved up the edges of her mouth as she waited.

"I told you that wouldn't take long," he said from behind her. Susan turned to discover he was dressed in a thick Irish cableknit sweater and dark slacks.

Smiling, she held her arm out to him. "Now I look like something the cat dragged in. I wish you'd said something before. I hate to meet anyone looking like this."

An arm around her shoulders firmly guided her out of the office. He paused to lock the door, placing a plain brown bag under his arm as he did so. Susan assumed the bag contained his clothes.

"To be honest, I don't think Joey will notice."

"Joey?"

"A leukemia patient of mine. He's going home

today, after a long stay at the hospital. Poor fellow's been through quite a bit, and I wanted to stop in and see him before he's released. Interested?"

From the look in his eye Susan realized this wasn't an ordinary patient, but someone Adam cared about deeply. "You bet." No doubt Joey worshipped his doctor. As everyone else seemed to, if the bulletin board was any indication.

"If I ever get sick, can I make an appointment?" The question was asked in a teasing tone, but there was an underlying note of seriousness that Adam didn't fail to recognize.

The hesitation was enough to make Susan edgy.

"Of course," he said at last.

"I don't think you need to worry. I'm fit as a fiddle."

A hand slid over her hip and buttocks. "You can say that again," he said, his gaze dark and meaningful.

The hospital was only three short blocks from his office. Several people waved greetings as he walked up the front steps. Adam was cornered almost the minute he walked through the wide double doors onto the polished tile floor.

After brief introductions, the nurse, a white-haired older woman, engaged him in a series of questions. Adam flashed Susan an apologetic smile. She returned the gesture, assuring him she didn't mind. Ten minutes later he directed her to the pediatrics ward and into the nine-year-old's room.

"Hi, Joey."

"Dr. Gallagher," the youth responded with an enthusiastic smile, sitting up in bed.

He was dressed in *Star Wars* pajamas, and a watchman's cap adorned his bald head. Blue eyes sparkled with mischief as he directed his gaze toward Susan.

"This is my friend, Susan Mackenzie," Adam introduced, curving an arm around her shoulders.

"Hi, Susan." A huge smile revealed a wide space between two front teeth. Joey looked at Adam. "She's real pretty."

Something Susan couldn't define flickered across Adam's face.

"Congratulations, Joey. Dr. Gallagher tells me you're going to be released today."

"Honest?." Excitement vibrated through the boy as he turned his attention to Adam. "Do I really get to go home?"

"Seems that way," Adam admitted with a wry chuckle. "As much as the nurses would like to keep you, I thought it was time your mother had the chance to shower you with some of that attention."

"Yippee," he shouted. He threw his cap in the air, then made a wild dive to catch it before it fell onto the floor, which nearly sent him off the bed.

"Remember what we talked about before you had the chemotherapy?" Adam's eyes suddenly turned serious.

Some of the excitement faded from Joey's eyes. "I remember," he mumbled, glancing away. "I know I wasn't as good as I should have been, but I tried real hard."

"I know you did." Adam tossed a teasing glance to Susan. "Nurse Perkins and I talked it over, and I contacted a friend of mine. He wanted me to give you this." Opening the bag, Adam took out a baseball and handed it to Joey.

For a moment the boy stared at it with openmouthed disbelief. "Dave Winfield signed this?"

"I think he might have put your name on it there someplace."

"Wow." The one word was barely above a whisper as he reverently turned the ball over and over in his hand.

"But then the rest of the Yankees felt deprived after I told them about you, so they wanted me to give you this." Placing his hand inside the sack, Adam produced a leather mitt covered with autographs.

"Everyone on the whole team?" Joey raised questioning awe-filled eyes to Adam.

"It seems they don't hear about boys as brave as you all that often."

Tears shimmered in the blue eyes as Joey threw his arms around Adam's neck. "You've got to be the best doctor in the whole world."

Sometime later Susan sat across from Adam at a small Italian restaurant not far from the hospital.

"How'd you manage that?"

"What?" he asked, looking over the top of the menu.

"The autographed baseball and mitt."

A wry grin drove grooves into the sides of his mouth. "Don't ask. I owe so many people favors for that one, I may be giving free exams until the year 2000."

"You don't know Dave Winfield?"

"Heavens no," he admitted with a chuckle.

"You really love that little boy, don't you?" The question was unnecessary, the answer obvious, but she wanted to watch Adam when he admitted it, praying she'd see the same look in his face when he looked at her one day.

"I do. There aren't many people I admire more than Joey Williams."

"Is he going to make it?"

"Yes." The lone word was issued forcefully, as if the strength of Adam's will would be enough to heal him. "What would you like to order?"

They'd barely had time to look at the menu, and Susan realized he didn't want her to question him about the boy. Doing a quick survey of the dishes listed, Susan quirked her mouth thoughtfully. If she were Rosemary, she'd order the salad. "The lasagna," she said with a determination that caused Adam to look at her curiously.

He ordered two of the same when the waitress came to their table.

Everything was delicious, just as Adam had claimed it would be. When their dishes were cleared away and the girl refreshed their cups of coffee, Susan glanced at her watch and sighed with disappointment.

"What's wrong?" Adam asked, both hands cupped around his coffee cup.

"I've got to get home. I didn't even tell Rosemary I was going to be gone. We're supposed to attend a party this afternoon. Do you know Charlie Johnson?"

Adam shook his head. Susan didn't suppose he would.

"He's a friend."

"In publishing?" The casual interest was a pose.

Susan was intensely aware that Adam was more than curious.

"Yes," she said, and breathed heavily. This was the time when she'd sit in eager anticipation to see if Adam would follow true to pattern. Would he make the suggestion that they meet again? He hadn't in the past, and she'd been left wondering.

Replacing her cup in the saucer, she glanced at Adam. He seemed to be lost in his own thoughts. "Adam?" she whispered, then bit into her lip to keep from asking. Hadn't she promised herself she wouldn't?

He looked up expectantly. "Yes?"

She shrugged her shoulders lightly. "Nothing," she said, and glanced down. A long strand of dark hair fell forward, and she looped it around her ear.

"Susan." Her name was spoken softly.

Eagerly she looked up. "Yes?"

"There's another game next Saturday. Would you like to come?"

"Adam Gallagher," she cried happily. "I could kiss you."

Chapter Four

Panting, her breath coming in ragged gasps, Rosemary Thomas let herself into the apartment. Susan looked up expectantly from her position on the sofa.

"My goodness, you really are taking this physical fitness stuff seriously."

Beads of perspiration poured down Rosemary's face as she gave a weak nod and staggered into the bathroom, returning a minute later with a hand towel to wipe her face. Collapsing onto the carpet, she attempted to speak, but the sounds she emitted were barely recognizable.

Concerned now, Susan set the cookbook aside and leaped to her bare feet. "Rosie, are you all right?"

An emphatic bob of the brown head assured Susan she was. "Wonderful," she gasped.

Hurrying into the kitchen, Susan opened the refrigerator and took out a diet soda. "Here." She removed the pull tab and handed the soft drink to her friend.

"Are you crazy?" Rosemary choked, and looked at her with wide-eyed disgust. "I'm not going to poison my body with that junk."

Susan looked from her friend to the soda and lightly shrugged. "Okay, then I will." Resuming her cross-legged position on the couch, she tipped her head back and took a large swig out of the aluminum can.

"Susan," Rosemary groaned. "I worry about you. I swear you'll be half-dead by age thirty. Look at you. Already your arteries are becoming clogged with cholesterol, and bags are beginning to form under your eyes."

"That's from so much reading," she returned, not in the least troubled.

Undaunted, Rosemary continued. "And physically, you're a wreck."

"That's not what Charlie Johnson said last week," she replied easily, then took another drink from the can.

Rosemary chose to ignore the comment. "Really, Susan, I'm worried."

"Don't be. I'm happy, and that's all that counts."

Groaning, Rosemary lay back on the carpet and took in huge gulps of air until her breathing returned to normal. "Aren't you going out tonight?" Glancing at her wristwatch, she looked back at Susan, her eyes questioning. "You've always got a date Friday night."

"No," she murmured without looking up from her book. There had been a couple of invitations, but she wanted to get to bed early for the sheer practicality of getting enough sleep for the game with Adam in the morning. "What about you and Carl?" she asked, keeping her place in the book with her finger as she glanced over to Rosemary.

"We're attending a lecture relating fiber in the diet to sound mental health."

Susan bit her lip to keep from saying something sarcastic but couldn't keep from rolling her eyes dramatically. More than once she suspected that Rosemary had become a health-food fanatic because it was the only common ground she shared with Carl, who was part owner of a gentlemen's gym. The two had dated steadily for over a month. Susan liked her roommate's friend, but somehow the picture of Rosemary and Carl as a couple didn't gel. Maybe if Rosemary hadn't been so eager to have Susan join her in the craziness, she could have looked at them in a different light.

"Scoff all you like. But Carl and I find that sort of discussion enthralling."

"I didn't say a word," Susan replied defensively.

"You didn't have to." Making a show of standing, Rosemary wrapped the towel around her neck and headed for the bathroom.

A few minutes later Susan heard the shower running. Her smile threatened to break into a full laugh. Fiber and mental health. Honestly!

After having read each cookie recipe, Susan decided to stick with her original choice, chocolate chip. Lining up the ingredients on top of the small formica counter, she blended the sugar and butter. She had just cracked

the eggs against the side of the bowl when Rosemary
sauntered in.

"What are you making?"

"Cookies." Susan looked up and smiled. "Hey, you
look nice."

Rosemary beamed her pleasure at the compliment.
"It's all part of the cardiovascular program Carl's
designed for me."

"Gee, and I thought it was the new dress," Susan
teased.

"You're not putting processed white sugar in those
cookies, are you?" She asked the question as if Susan
were about to add strychnine to the batter.

"Yup." She already knew what was coming.

"White sugar is the curse of America. Mark my
words, Miss Know-It-All, mark my words."

Again Susan had to bite her tongue, but she managed
to let it pass without comment.

A half hour later, Rosemary and Carl were on their
way and Susan was left alone in the apartment. That
she was the one sitting at home was definitely a switch.
Usually it was her own social calendar that was tightly
booked. She'd turned down several invitations since
meeting Adam. It wasn't that she didn't want to go out,
but that she'd rather go with him.

The entire week had passed without a word. Not that
she'd expected Adam to call. Expected, no; desperately hoped, yes. What was it about this one man that
made him so fascinating? More and more he dominated
her thoughts. It had become impossible not to compare
him with every other man she'd known and dated. In

every instance Adam came out better. True, he wasn't as good-looking as the others, but his appeal was by far stronger.

The alarm rang early the next morning, and Susan threw back the covers and immediately climbed out of bed. Feeling in an unusually chipper mood, she hummed softly as she dressed. A quick glance out the bedroom window revealed heavy clouds and a good possibility of rain. Instead of taking her leather jacket, she pulled on a beige belted raincoat and matching cloche. A pink hatbox contained the saucer-sized chocolate chip cookies she'd promised Adam she'd bring for the team.

"I must be dreaming." Rosemary said between two yawns, sitting up in bed and rubbing her eyes.

"Sorry, I didn't mean to wake you."

"You didn't. It was such a shock to hear you humming that it drove me straight out of bed. I mean, Susan Mackenzie, the original morning grouch! The girl who said if God had meant for man to see the sun rise, He would have made it happen later in the day. The same girl who needs two cups of coffee before she's civil."

"One and the same," she said with a wide smile, and tucked a thermos of coffee under her arm.

"It must be love," Rosemary said under her breath, and Susan was sure her friend hadn't meant for her to hear. In twenty-four years she couldn't remember having been happier, and it was all because she was on her way to Adam.

By the time she entered the park, a light sprinkle had begun to fall, dotting the ground. Brisk steps carried her to the soccer fields. But when she arrived, there wasn't anyone else around. Had the game been canceled? Surely Adam would have let her know, wouldn't he? Looking around, she noted a tall male figure walking toward her and felt a flood of relief. Until this moment she hadn't been aware how important it was that she see him this morning.

When he lifted his hand and waved, she returned the gesture and started walking toward him.

"Morning," she greeted cheerfully once he was within hearing distance. "What happened? Has the game been called?" Tiny waves of pleasure pulsed through her at the raw, virile sight he presented. He wore a tweed jacket and dark slacks, and Susan couldn't remember a time he looked more enticingly masculine.

"The other team forfeited the game."

"Oh." She tried to disguise her disappointment.

"I didn't know about it until yesterday afternoon," Adam said in a low-pitched voice.

"You should have said something. I brought the cookies."

"The cookies, damn. I'm sorry, I'd forgotten about them."

"No problem," she assured him. "Want one? There's coffee too."

"You think of everything." He took the hatbox and thermos out of her hand and led the way to a sheltered picnic area not far from the field. "I would have phoned last night," he said, placing the items on the picnic table, "but I thought you probably had a date." When he glanced up, his expression was bland and guarded.

"I did," she said, her meaningful gaze meeting his. "In the kitchen making cookies. And since I went to all this trouble, the least you can do is eat every last one of them."

"Then I will." A smile brightened his face, and a happy light gleamed from the dark depths of his eyes. "Hey, these are good. You didn't tell me you could cook."

"I have talents you've only begun to discover, Adam Gallagher." She didn't really mind that he hadn't phoned, knowing that she probably wouldn't have seen him if he had.

"That I don't doubt." His voice was husky and filled with a sweet intensity that made her glance up.

Turning her around and into his arms, he placed a hand along the side of her neck and tilted her head back with the subtle pressure of one finger.

Susan's breath became shallow. Anticipating his kiss, she parted her mouth willingly and slipped her arms around his neck as she yielded to the mastery of his power over her senses. The kiss lingered and lingered as if they were both unwilling for the intimacy to end. When he buried his face against the slim column of her neck, Susan moaned, not wanting him to stop. She trembled, afraid he would pull away from her again, mentally more than physically. She couldn't bear it. Lifting herself onto tiptoe, she arched against him, her hands clinging to his neck. One kiss and the whole crazy world took a tailspin.

Adam raised his head, and his thumb lightly traced her throbbing mouth.

"I need some of that coffee," he said finally.

"Why?" Susan asked in confusion, knowing it would feel cold outside of his arms.

"Because we're in the middle of Central Park on a Saturday morning and are about to be joined by half of New York City."

"Oh, of course," she said, and dropped her hands just in time to see several runners dressed in various outfits enthusiastically jog past. "What was that?"

"Runners." Adam's voice was full of contained amusement.

"They jog in packs now?" As far as Susan knew, Rosemary ran alone. "And just where do these herds graze?"

"Do I detect a sarcastic note?" Adam asked. His mouth quivered, and Susan knew he was fighting a smile. "Don't be so hard on us."

"Us?"

"Sure, I'm a runner. I thought you knew."

"No," she said, and breathed softly. "No, I didn't. When do you run?"

"Weekdays right here in the park. I usually follow the same route as everyone else. Two and a half miles is all I have time for, but I love it."

Susan could recall a time she'd thought he was a soccer player, but what a natural runner he must be. His long strides would display a pantherlike grace. Already her mind was buzzing. Perhaps Rosemary wasn't so crazy after all. Maybe it was time she thought about joining the physical fitness craze.

"You look a million miles away."

"Oh, sorry." She snapped herself out of her private thoughts. Lowering herself beside Adam on the bench, she opened the thermos and poured out the steaming coffee. "We'll have to drink from the same cup and share all those disgusting germs."

His gaze was warm and teasing. "I think my immunity system can take that."

He reached for a cookie and handed it to Susan before taking another for himself.

"Hey, I was only teasing. You don't have to eat them all. Save some for next week."

"Next week?" He looked at her blankly.

"Yes, coach, remember your team. The game's soccer."

Adam took a sip of the coffee and placed the red plastic cup within easy reach for her. "I guess I forgot to tell you today's game was the last one of the season."

Disappointment washed over her. How quickly Saturdays had come to be special, knowing she would meet Adam. Now that was over. "Yes, I guess you did." The realization was a threatening one. "Do you coach anything else?"

He flashed her a brief smile. "Only soccer. I don't have time for anything else."

Was he saying he didn't have time for her either?

"You can keep the cookies then."

"I have no intention of giving them up," he said. His gaze slid to Susan, and she realized he was referring to more than the cookies.

It may have been a raining, depressing and yucky morning, but Susan couldn't recall a more glorious

day. "Are you going to treat me to a decent breakfast?"

"I imagine that could be arranged."

"First thing we're going to do is take you to the
health-food store and introduce you to Fred. He'll set
you up on a vitamin program." Rosemary's deep
brown eyes gleamed with enthusiasm.

"I want to start running. Not once did I mention
taking vitamins."

Placing one hand on her hip in challenge, Rosemary
sighed meaningfully. "You've got to learn to trust me,
Susan. Without the proper vitamin fortification, you
could be desperately sick within a week."

"How much is this going to cost me?" Susan demanded, mentally calculating the fifty dollars she had
already spent for a multishaded turquoise running suit.

"Does your health have a price?"

"This month, yes," she returned forcefully.

"Okay, okay. We'll start with the bare essentials."
Rosemary was at the height of her glory. Susan had
trouble restraining a laugh. Her friend seemed to
believe it had been her influence that had changed
Susan's thinking. And Susan was her first convert.

An hour later she looked over the balance in her
checkbook and knew she'd barely have enough to live
on for the rest of the month. Rosemary's bare essentials consisted of five bottles of high-potency vitamins.
She did have to admit that Rosemary's friend, Fred,
had been helpful and friendly. In her eagerness, Rosemary had assembled twenty different minerals and
vitamins she considered indispensable. Fred had nar-

rowed the field, helping Susan stay within a reasonable price range.

Their next stop had been the grocery store. By the time they arrived at the check-out stand, Susan was staring at the items with a sense of disbelief. Tofu, yogurt, sunflower seeds, cottage cheese, fresh fruit and vegetables. No potato chips, no diet soda, nothing that so much as hinted of processed white sugar or flour.

"Hot dogs!" Susan exclaimed. "I forgot the hot dogs."

"Never," Rosemary cried righteously. "They're pure poison."

Defeated, Susan shook her head numbly. "Yes, but they taste so good."

"Wait until you've had tofu spread thick across a stone-ground wheat cracker," Rosemary countered. "That's what good is all about."

A multitude of doubts surfaced, but Susan left them unvoiced.

The first alarm rang early Monday morning. Snuggling contentedly under her blankets, Susan rolled over, assured of another hour of sleep. Rosemary spent the early morning doing her exercises and left early to walk to work.

"Susan," the soft voice broke into her dream.

"Humm," she purred, pulling the sheet closer to her ear.

"Time to get up."

"No it's not," she mumbled.

"If you're going to become physically fit, then the best way to start is with walking."

The thought passed fleetingly through her mind that sleep was of more value than exercise. But the warm vision of being with Adam every morning, even if it meant running, was enough inducement for her to struggle to a sitting position.

"Here." Dressed in shorts and a T-shirt, Rosemary cheerfully handed her a steaming mug.

Susan forced one eye open, not awake enough to thank her friend. Bless Rosemary's heart, she mused, forcing a poor facsimile of a smile across her face.

Susan took one sip and spit the horrible-tasting liquid back into the cup. "Good Lord, what is this stuff?" she cried distastefully. A shudder ran through her at the unfamiliar taste.

"Seeped parsley leaves," Rosemary returned proudly. "It's just the thing to get the ol' juices flowing in the morning."

"Parsley?" Susan handed the cup back to her friend. "I've got to have coffee."

"It's all in your head," Rosemary said with a certainty that sounded irrefutable.

Susan staggered into the kitchen, poured water into the pot, scooped grounds from the container and turned on the stove.

"You can't," Rosemary insisted. "The caffeine in one cup will undo everything we're trying to . . ."

One fiery glare was enough to sufficiently convince Rosemary that maybe this was one point on which it would be best to compromise.

Twenty minutes later, Susan stared at her friend incredulously. Rosemary had completed one hundred and fifty sit-ups, Susan fifteen. An equal number of jumping jacks had been done by Rosemary with an ease that shocked Susan, who had managed twenty-five.

"How do you feel?" Rosemary shouted, hands on her hips as she lifted her knees while running in place.

"Like I should quit while I'm ahead."

"That's probably not a bad idea. Don't make the mistake of doing too much at once."

"There's little fear of that," Susan said with a laugh, and realized that although she wasn't about to give up her morning cup of coffee, she didn't mind the exercise.

"Didn't I tell you this is great!" Rosemary shouted, still running, her knees coming up higher and higher.

"Yes, you did," Susan admitted. "How long before I'll be ready to jog?"

"Depends on how far you want to go?"

She shrugged, hoping her friend would believe the figure came off the top of her head. "I don't know, two miles, two and a half at the most."

"That'll take weeks."

"Weeks?" Susan cried. She couldn't wait that long. True to character, Adam hadn't set a time to see her again. It had only been two days since she'd met him in the park, and already she was worried. "I've got to be able to hit the streets faster than that."

"Why?" Rosemary stopped, taking in huge breaths and slowly sauntering around the room before placing her hands on her knees and bending forward.

"Well . . . because." Her mind struggled for a plausible excuse. "I just want too, that's all."

"I don't suppose this has anything to do with Adam, does it?"

A denial rose automatically to her lips, but she refused to let it escape. "What makes you ask?"

Wiping her face with a hand towel, Rosemary gave her an odd look. "We've been living together for almost two years. I know you. I've seen men come and go. But I've never seen you act like this over any one of them."

"I've never felt this strong about anyone else." Her gaze leveled with her friend's. "I learned last week that Adam's a runner."

A look of understanding flashed over Rosemary's face with a clarity that was unmistakable. "Ah, now I get the picture."

"Good, how long will it be before I'm capable of holding my own on a two-and-a-half-mile course."

Rosemary's eyes widened and she shrugged helplessly. "Weeks."

"I can't wait that long," she said with a groan.

"There isn't any way you'd be able to get in top physical condition any sooner."

"Who said top condition? I'd be willing to settle for breathing normally while doing sit-ups."

Rosemary's laugh echoed from the bathroom as she strolled inside and turned on the shower.

A week later, Susan was almost desperate. It'd been ten days since she'd last seen Adam, and she hadn't heard a word from him. In the past when she'd been uncertain over their relationship, she'd had trouble sleeping. That was no longer the case. Rosemary had devised a workout program that left Susan exhausted. Every night she crawled into bed and fell into an easy slumber.

Within six days Susan was matching Rosemary in sit-ups and jumping jacks. Although she wasn't thrilled about the two-and-a-half-mile walk to the Simon and Schuster Building in Rockefeller Center, she faithfully made the trek each morning. For, as hard as she had berated her roommate's enthusiasm for physical fitness, Susan found she enjoyed it—not the early-morning hours, or even the exertion, but the overall good feeling afterward. Rosemary claimed it was the endorphins. Susan didn't know what it was.

Wednesday morning she woke at five-thirty, long before the alarm sounded. Lying on her back and staring at the ceiling, she released a slow, quivering breath. Wouldn't Adam ever phone? Hadn't he guessed how much he meant to her? Nothing seemed to be going right. Tuesday afternoon she'd had an argument with an agent that had weighed on her mind all night. Now, in the darkness that preceded the first light, Susan realized it wasn't that she wanted to see Adam; she needed to see him. Needed him.

Without questioning the wisdom of her actions, she laid back the covers and quietly slipped out of bed. Making the least amount of noise possible, she took the running outfit hanging in the closet and tiptoed into the bathroom. With any luck she'd be out the door before Rosemary knew she was gone.

Although the morning was crisp and the sky dark, several runners were already in the park. Susan knew enough not to take a coat. She'd be warm as soon as she started jogging. But until she saw Adam and joined with him, she'd have to suffer the cold. Limbering up on her way to the soccer fields, she jiggled her arms at her sides and made a pretense of the same with her legs. Jogging shouldn't be so difficult; after all, she'd been walking the same distance every morning with Rosemary. Running couldn't be that different. Now all she needed was a little luck. She had no idea what time Adam ran, but she'd noted that his office hours weren't until midmorning and assumed he did hospital rounds before then. So if he ran every morning, it had to be around six. All she had to do was wait around by the picnic area until he came into view and she could casually join him.

Fifteen minutes later, Susan stood shivering and miserable, convinced that Adam wasn't coming. With her arms cradling her midsection, she didn't know how she would ever manage to give the impression she'd "accidentally" run into him.

"Susan." Her name was shouted from the distance and she had to squint to see the source. Adam! It took all her restraint not to run and throw herself into his arm.

"Hi," she called, and waved, forcing herself to smile cheerfully. Her mouth felt cold and brittle. If she didn't start moving soon she'd freeze to death. Trotting toward him, she hoped he was impressed with the color-coordinated jogging outfit.

"I didn't know you ran?" He slowed his pace to match hers.

"Yes," she mumbled, already feeling breathless. Rosemary had told her the first few minutes were always the worst. "Since I hadn't heard from you, I thought maybe I'd join you once around the reservoir and see how you've been."

"Great, and you?"

"Wonderful," she lied. Just once, couldn't he tell her he'd been thinking of her? That he'd missed her last Saturday? Her lungs were beginning to hurt, and she struggled to maintain the pace. Talking and breathing were almost impossible.

"How many miles do you run a week?" Adam said, breaking the silence.

"Ten." Somehow she managed to get out the one word. She didn't have the breath to explain that she usually walked the distance.

"Have you ever averaged your minutes per mile?"

"No." Centering her vision on the pavement in front of her, she concentrated on placing one foot in front of the other, nothing more. She wasn't going to embarrass herself. She'd finish the course if it killed her. Her lungs felt as if they were on fire, the pain extending up her throat as she took in ragged breaths. Every muscle in her legs was screaming in protest. At just the moment Susan was convinced she was either going to faint, vomit or die, Adam came to a stop.

Hands on his hips, he tipped his head back and took several deep breaths. "Wow, that felt good."

Susan didn't respond. Instead she collapsed onto the wet ground, her entire body feeling like a limp rubber band.

Adam joined her on the dew-covered grass. Susan didn't mind the moisture; it felt cool and comforting against her burning flesh.

"You okay?" Concern drove creases into his wide brow as his face appeared above hers.

She didn't even have the breath to assure him.

Nodding her head and waving her hand was the most she could offer.

"I imagine my pace is a bit faster than yours. I like to maintain seven-minute miles. I imagine we were doing eight, maybe a nine-minute mile."

"Oh," was all she could manage.

A hand brushed a long strand of hair from her temple and lingered. "It's good to see you." The intensity in his look created a tidal wave of emotions within her. Every painful step of the run was worth that one tender look.

She struggled to sit up. If he wouldn't say it, she would. "I missed you."

"I was going to call," he murmured, and looked away.

"Why didn't you?" she whispered, hoping to hide the hurt and disappointment in her voice.

"You're an extremely attractive woman." There was a ragged edge to his voice that hadn't been there when jogging.

"That's an excuse?" Had she misread his look that day when he'd told her he had no intention of letting her go?

"Susan," he said, then paused and dragged in a deep breath. "I'm not a plain-looking man. People are going to take a look at us and see beauty and the beast. I don't think . . ."

"Stop it, stop it right now." A reserve of energy she hadn't known existed loaned her voice the strength to shout at him. "Don't you ever say that to me again." Raising herself up so that she was on her knees, she jabbed a finger into the muscular wall of his chest.

"You are the most attractive, wonderful, fun person I know, and if I ever hear you talk like that about yourself or me again, I'll . . . I'll . . ." She didn't know what she'd do. "I'll scream," she added finally.

"You're managing to do a fair job of that now." He glanced around him self-consciously, his look showing he was grateful that there weren't many others nearby.

"I know what I'll do," she cried desperately. "I'll scar myself and then maybe you won't look at me like I'm Miss Perfect . . . or Gail. That was her name, wasn't it? Then maybe you'll treat me like a normal woman—like everyone else treats me." She recognized how irrational she sounded, but she was hurt and resentful and had said the first thing that came into her head.

A muscle jerked angrily in his jaw, and Susan knew she had gone too far. He didn't like her to mention Gail. What was so sacred about his long-lost love? If he still cared for his college sweetheart, Susan thought she'd die.

"Have you ever stopped to think that maybe I didn't want to see you?" he demanded in a low growl. The line of his jaw was hard, the look in his eyes almost savage.

The words hurt more than if he'd slammed his fist into her stomach. For a stunned second she didn't breathe. Tears filled her eyes and she lowered her gaze, not wanting him to know the power he had to hurt her. Crying was the final humiliation; if he saw that it would be too much.

"No, I guess I hadn't." She whispered the words in a husky, pain-filled murmur. Wearily she stood, her back to him. "I'm sorry, I won't bother you again." By the time she made it to the outskirts of the park, her vision had become a watery blur and she hardly knew where she was walking.

Pausing outside her apartment door, she wiped the tears from her face, then let herself in.

"Susan," Rosemary cried. "Where have you been? I was worried." She stopped abruptly. "Susan . . . you're crying." She sounded shocked.

"Go to work without me today, will you?" Susan asked, keeping her face averted. "Tell Karen I'm sick. Maybe I'll be in later . . . if I feel better."

"Sure." The one word was whispered soothingly. "Are you going to be all right?"

"No." She tried to laugh. "But you go on, I'll live."

"You're sure?"

She wasn't, but she gave a weak nod.

Rosemary left a few minutes later and Susan sank onto the couch, bringing up her knees and cradling them with her arms. Her chin was tucked against her breast as the recriminations washed over her. Why couldn't she leave well enough alone? Why couldn't she have waited until Adam contacted her? He would have eventually.

Someone banged on her door. The sound reverberated around the silent room and her head shot up. Adam? No, she decided. If he'd just finished telling her he didn't want to see her, then he wasn't likely to follow. Besides, he had his hospital rounds to do.

"Yes." She unlocked the door and quickly opened it. Her gaze collided with Adam's as his presence loomed before her.

Chapter Five

✽

"Susan, I'm sorry." He didn't bother with a greeting. "I didn't mean what I said." After a brief hesitation he reached out and touched her shoulder.

Susan didn't need any more encouragement. Wordlessly, she walked into his arms and buried her face in his chest. His deep breathing stirred the hair at the crown of her head, and she closed her eyes to the healing balm his embrace offered.

"Why?" The sound of her voice was muffled by the strength of his hold. Susan didn't need to explain further. She had made a fool of herself from the beginning with Adam. Never before had she waited around for a man to ask her out. No one else in the world could have induced her to push herself beyond her physical capabilities just for the opportunity to see him.

Two large hands cupped her face as his gaze probed hers. Susan noted a curious pain that tinged his eyes.

"You're so beautiful."

For the first time in her life, being attractive was a detriment. With anyone else it would have been a plus. An involuntary protest slipped from her lips. "Adam, please," she said, and groaned. "I'm not."

"Enough for anyone to question what someone like you is doing with me."

"That's nonsense." She wasn't angry. Strangely, she felt devoid of emotion, as if the tears had depleted her. Raising her own hand, she cupped his and turned her head so that she could press a kiss into his palm.

A sound came from deep in his throat as his mouth descended to hers, plundering her ready lips with a kiss that was fierce and hungry. Gradually the hard pressure lessened to a gentle possession as his mouth moved lazily over hers. The longings, the yearnings he created within her left Susan trembling. Again she was a willing victim to the sweet, rapturous intensity of this man.

"When I'm with you," he began, his voice slightly uneven, "I think I'm the luckiest man in the world. I treasure every minute and die every time we say good-bye."

Susan couldn't believe what she was hearing. "But why don't you ever call me afterward? Why do you leave me lost and uncertain, waiting to hear from you?"

"That's the way I feel when we're together," he admitted dryly.

He held her tight, his chin resting on the top of her

head. Susan wished she could look at him, watch him as he spoke.

"Later I realize you've probably got plenty of men wanting to date you."

"I don't," she murmured, and heaved a troubled sigh. What would it take to convince Adam she wasn't turning away hordes of men to be with him?

"Well, if not, then there's something wrong with half the population of New York City."

"Oh, Adam."

"I wish I had a dime for every time I picked up the phone to call you or all the times I've found myself standing outside your apartment building. Then I stop and realize you'd be crazy to be interested in someone like me."

"I admit it then," she told him forcefully. "I'm crazy, because I'm interested in you, Adam Gallagher. I'm very interested. Now is that plain enough for you, or do you need more convincing?"

His soft chuckle mussed her hair. "That'll probably hold me until I get downstairs. I'm not the most secure person when it comes to romantic involvements. I don't know if that's a result of Gail or just being homely."

"I wish you'd stop saying that," she said, and released an angry breath. "You are not ugly! I find you so attractive, I don't know what to do or say to convince you."

"When you're in my arms, I don't need anything else. It comes after a long day at the office and I find that I want to share my day with you. Then I realize I can't bore someone like you with something so trivial."

"Yesterday I had an argument with an agent. The

woman was wrong and unreasonable, and my afternoon was ruined. All I could think about afterward was how much I wanted to be with you. I probably wouldn't have said a word about her or the disagreement, but I needed you."

"Next weekend—"

"Yes," she interrupted with a small laugh.

"Yes what?"

"I'll go, no matter what it is or where it's at. I want to be with you every weekend for a long time."

"Litchfield, Connecticut?"

"Timbucktu."

"Susan," he groaned, "I mean it."

"So do I," she whispered lovingly.

"Some friends of mine are getting together for the weekend. We'll be staying with my mother, who'll probably force you to look at baby pictures of me."

"I'll love it."

His grip tightened as his mouth moved roughly over her hair. "Do you want to meet again tomorrow morning?"

"You mean"—she swallowed tightly—"to run?"

"Sure."

Susan wasn't about to refuse.

"Only this time let's complete the full loop. We only went a mile today."

"Robe?" Rosemary called from the bedroom.

"Check," Susan said with a happy laugh.

"Toothbrush?"

"Got it."

"Is there anything you haven't got?"

"Not lately," Susan admitted with a contented sigh.

Rosemary glanced over at the two pieces of luggage sitting beside the door. "Are you sure you're just going for the weekend? I've seen you pack less for a six-day conference."

"I know." Susan smiled ruefully. "But Adam said something about dinner and dancing Saturday night, and I couldn't decide what to wear so I packed three outfits."

Not for the first time that week, Susan noted the distant look in her friend's eyes. "Is everything all right, Rosie?"

"Sure," she replied flippantly, and turned away.

"Are you sure there isn't something wrong between you and Carl."

"Nothing's right between us," she returned flatly.

"I'm sorry." Susan's look was sympathetic. She couldn't help feeling her friend's unhappiness, but she wasn't all that surprised. Almost from the beginning Susan had thought that Rosemary's and Carl's personalities didn't mesh.

"Well, at least one of us is happy," Rosemary added with a meaningful shrug.

There hadn't been a time in her life when Susan was more pleased with the way her life was going. Every morning she met Adam and somehow, by the grace of God, managed the two-and-a-half-mile run. Usually they jogged at a much slower pace than Adam would have elected. But he was content to be at her side no matter how slowly she ran. Twice he'd phoned her for no particular reason other than to chat. And Thursday they met after work for a drink. After the lonely weeks of waiting for Adam to contact her, the last one had been heaven. Susan couldn't have been more excited about the weekend trip to Litchfield if she had been going on her honeymoon.

Adam was equally elated as he tucked her suitcases under his arm and leaned over to lightly brush his mouth over her lips. "Ready?"

"I think so." Her eyes smiled warmly into his. Turning, she flashed Rosemary a smile. "Take care. I probably won't be back until late Sunday."

"No problem," Rosemary said, and waved. "Have a good time, you two."

"We plan on it," Adam answered for them both.

This was the first time Susan had seen Adam's car, a year-old station wagon.

"To haul the soccer team," he explained when she arched a delicate brow questioningly.

The drive to Adam's hometown took almost four hours; they had stopped for dinner and leisurely prolonged the journey, waiting until the heavy weekend traffic thinned out.

"You'll like my mother," Adam told her, his free hand cupping hers as they headed back onto the freeway from the restaurant.

"I know I'll love her." *How can I help it when I already love her son?* Susan added silently. Her gaze fell on Adam as he drove, his profile illuminated by the headlights of oncoming cars. The beams flickered over the uneven planes of his face, blunt, hard features that looked as if someone had carved him out of wood. Facial contours that did little to reveal the gentle character of this wonderful man. Watching him, Susan's heart swelled with pride and a love so strong it stole her breath.

Apparently Adam felt her close study. He turned and gave her a smile that caused her heart to leap. "Happy?" he questioned as his hand squeezed hers gently.

"Oh, yes."

"I think I should warn you. My mother's bound to ask us a lot of embarrassing questions. She's a true romantic and would like to see me married and giving her a passel of grandchildren to spoil."

Susan's heartbeat raced to double time. If Adam proposed, she'd accept without a second's hesitation. "I think I can handle that; don't worry about it." She hoped her voice didn't relay the path her thoughts had taken. In the past she had chased after Adam embarrassingly, but when it came to a proposal of marriage, it would have to come from him. She didn't want him teasing their children someday about . . . Their children. The thought came so quickly, so naturally, that it put a halt to everything else. Her sight, hearing, breathing—the thought of being a wife and mother hurled her right out of reality. It took her a moment to realize Adam was talking and she hadn't heard a word he'd said.

"I'm sorry, I didn't catch that," she mumbled, looking over at him.

"I was just saying that I didn't doubt you could handle my mother's curiosity. If you can deal with pesky agents and finicky authors, my mother will be a snap."

Susan clenched her hands together tightly when

Adam exited from the freeway and entered a residential district of middle-class homes. No sooner had he parked the wagon in front of large two-story house with a huge porch than the front door flew open.

"Ready?" Adam whispered.

"I think so." One look told Susan she was going to like Adam's mother. There was no difficulty identifying the two as family. Each possessed the same wide forehead and the long, narrow face. Adam's mother was tall; her hair was completely white and pinned at the base of her neck in a small bun. The dark eyes twinkled delightedly as her gaze fell from Adam to Susan.

"Mom's going to love you," he said, and gave her arm a reassuring squeeze before opening the car door and climbing out. He held a hand to Susan, who scooted out his side. Immediately he pulled her to him as if making an unspoken statement about their relationship.

Gently he hugged his mother, then curved an arm around Susan's shoulders. "Mom, I'd like you to meet Susan Mackenzie. We're good friends."

The whitehaired woman pushed her glasses to the end of her nose and beamed Susan a warm smile. "Anytime my son brings a girl home to meet his mother, she's more than a friend. Welcome to Litchfield, Susan."

"Thank you."

With one arm around Susan and another around his mother's thick waist, Adam escorted them both into the house. The front door opened to a wide hallway. The living room was to the right and had a fire crackling in the fireplace. The stairway was to their immediate left, and the homey kitchen directly in front of them.

"I imagine you're starved," Adam's mother said, tucking a stray hair into the small bun. "Adam, why don't you bring in the luggage. Susan can have your sister's room. And Susan, you come with me so we can get to know one another."

Adam gave her a reassuring smile and winked. Dutifully she followed his mother into the kitchen, which was surprisingly large. A round oak table with claw feet was set in the middle with a freshly pressed linen cloth.

"You have a lovely home, Mrs. Gallagher."

"Olivia," she corrected gently. "I suppose I should think about selling out and moving into one of those fancy condominiums. But this has been home almost forty years now, and I can't see myself living anywhere else."

"My mom and dad are the same way."

After taking down mugs from the polished cupboards, Olivia turned and gestured toward the table. "Sit down and make yourself at home. I baked Adam's favorite deep-dish apple pie, which he'll manage to eat up in the time he's here. Would you like a piece?"

Susan was about to refuse. It had only been a short time since dinner. "Yes, please," she found herself agreeing. "Can I help?"

"No. You just make yourself comfortable. I'll join you in a minute."

Adam sauntered into the kitchen and kissed his mother on the cheek. "The luggage is safely delivered.

Is there anyplace else you'd like me to disappear to so you can barrage Susan with questions?"

Keeping a straight face, his mother turned. "Get the ice cream out of the basement freezer, would you please, Adam?"

"I don't like ice cream on my pie," he protested.

"I know, but I do. Now be away with you."

The minute Adam was out the back door, Olivia turned and shared a conspiratorial smile with Susan. "I really am pleased you've come. He needs someone."

"I like him very much."

"How'd you meet?" she questioned as she set coffee mugs and apple pie on the table. She pulled out a chair and sat beside Susan.

"At a party," Adam came in and answered for her. "You remember Ralph Jordan, don't you, Mother?"

"Ralph Jordan, Ralph Jordan." Olivia Gallagher repeated the name as if turning it over and over in her mind. "Of course, that college friend of yours. He's in publishing, isn't he?"

"Literary agent. He recently opened his own agency. He gave a party to celebrate. That's where Susan and I met; she's an editor."

"Associate editor," Susan corrected between swallows. "This pie is great." She dipped her fork into the flaky crust and leaned forward slightly to take another bite.

A pleased smile tugged at the corners of Olivia's mouth, denting crescent-shaped grooves along the side her face. "I'll give you the recipe if you like," she offered.

"I would," Susan accepted, and noticed the shocked look in Adam's eyes. He opened his mouth and closed it, giving his mother a perplexed look.

"You're meeting Lenny, Burt and Gary tomorrow night?" his mother asked. "This get-together is coming to be an annual thing with you four, isn't it?"

"Unless we make the time, we'll never see one another."

Adam had explained they were meeting his best high-school friends when he asked her to accompany him. From what she could remember, Lenny was a used-car salesman, Burt an electrician, and Gary a lawyer. The four had gone all the way through school together, and Gary on to college with Adam. Susan didn't need to be told that Adam was the kind of man who took friendship seriously. He didn't easily oblige himself to others, but when he did that commitment was total. If only she could find a way to explain to him that it was this kind dedication that made him so special to her. She was tired of dating self-centered, self-satisfying men who never looked past her face.

The three didn't move beyond the kitchen until it was late. Susan enjoyed the teasing banter exchanged between mother and son and nearly laughed out loud as Olivia brought out the family picture album as Adam had threatened she would.

"Mother," he admonished sharply, "Susan isn't interested in seeing that."

"Yes, I am," she contradicted, and flashed Adam a cheeky grin. "I know darn good and well that when you meet my parents, my mother is going to do the same thing." Her voice had dipped slightly; she hoped to convey the message that she planned on introducing him to her family. It wasn't a question of "if, but when."

"Next thing I know, Mom will have you reading all those silly books she treasures," Adam returned, and he gave a short derisive snort.

"Do you read romances?" Olivia studied Susan.

"All the time." When she'd first met Adam, Susan hadn't told him who employed her. All Adam knew was that she was an associate editor. He had no idea she worked for Silhouette.

"I knew a sweet girl like you would read romance novels."

Adam mumbled something under his breath that Susan couldn't make out.

"Mom's addicted to those things. I think she belongs to two or three of those book clubs."

"And what harm does it do?" his mother shot back defensively. "I can sit down and throw away the problems of the world and feel young again."

"Hogwash."

Enjoying this all the more, Susan hid a smile. "Do you enjoy Silhouettes?"

"I love them," Olivia returned enthusiastically. "I get the Romances and the Special Editions."

"Susan, you don't honestly read those things, do you?" Adam regarded her seriously. His eyes narrowed, forcing crinkling lines about his eyes and mouth as his expression developed into a troubled frown.

"Of course I do," she said with a reassuring smile. "I work for Silhouette."

"You're an editor for Silhouette?" he echoed disbelievingly, and rammed a hand through his hair. "A romance editor?" He murmured the question. "Why didn't you say something before now?"

"It never came up."

"A romance editor from Silhouette. Well, I'll be." Olivia looked at Susan as if she were sitting next to a famous movie star. "You must know all the authors."

"We have a wonderful group of authors, all excellent writers in addition to being wonderful people." Her mind wasn't on what she was saying to Olivia, but on the strange look that had come over Adam. She watched as the color drained from his face, his look remote, disturbed.

He excused himself a few minutes later. Susan's eyes followed him as he left the kitchen. What was wrong? What had she said that had upset him so much?

Olivia's gaze followed Susan's. "You love my son, don't you?"

"Very much," she told her honestly.

"He's been hurt," the older woman explained.

Dropping her gaze, Susan cupped the empty mug with both hands. "He told me about Gail. I know how much she meant to him."

"You'd never do that to him," Olivia said knowingly. "I knew the minute you climbed out of the car how you two felt about one another. Has he told you he's in love with you?"

"Not yet," she whispered achingly.

A hand reached across and gave Susan a reassuring squeeze. "He will; just be patient."

A sad smile touched her eyes. "Patience is one thing

Adam's teaching me. I knew how I felt about him almost from the beginning, but he's unsure. It's been only in the last week that we've been seeing one another regularly."

"He's not unsure," his mother countered. "Only cautious. Once burned, twice shy."

"But I'm not Gail."

"Deep down he knows that. It'll take some time for him to openly admit how he feels. After he does he'll never give you reason to doubt again."

Susan's worried expression softened. "I'm not giving up on him, not by a long shot. That guy is stuck with me whether he likes it or not."

They talked for a few minutes longer, and Susan helped Olivia clear off the table. Adam wasn't in the living room and Susan assumed he'd gone up to bed. Feeling frustrated and a little hurt, she sat and chatted with his mother for another hour. When Olivia yawned, Susan made the pretense of being tired herself. Olivia led her up the stairs to the room where Susan would be sleeping. The door opposite hers was closed. Olivia glanced at it, frowned and gestured with one hand.

"I thought I'd taught my son better manners than this."

"Please don't be angry. I'm sure he's very tired."

"I won't have company making excuses for my son. If he was ten years younger, I'd take him over my knee and spank him good and proper."

The mental picture produced a weak smile. "Good night, Olivia, and thank you." She hesitated momentarily. "When we drove up to the house tonight, Adam told me I was going to like you. He was right." Impulsively, she gave the woman a small hug.

It was no use sleeping. Susan changed into her long silk gown and pulled on the pink velvet robe and matching slippers. Sitting on top of the single bed, she couldn't help wonder what had gone wrong. What had she said? The only thing she could possibly attribute his anger to was the fact that she was a romance editor. But why should that upset him? It didn't make sense. Nothing did with Adam. Would she ever understand him? They'd been so happy. Dear God, she prayed, don't let it be ruined. Not when she'd come this far.

A half hour later Susan heard a noise downstairs. She sat up, uncertain. Both she and Olivia had assumed Adam had gone to bed because the wagon was parked outside. But had he?

Gently laying aside her covers, she climbed out of the bed and stuck her feet into the slippers. Tying the sash of her housecoat, she carefully opened the bedroom door. A dim light illuminated the stairway. Noiselessly, Susan moved down the stairs. Halfway down she paused.

Adam was sitting in the living room, slumped forward, his face buried in his hands. He looked as if a great weariness had settled over him and he was friendless and discouraged. A sadness possessed him, a hurt he would never share. As if aware someone was watching him, he straightened and turned his head. Their eyes met and locked. Susan's stomach knotted into a ball of pain at the look she had come to recognize in Adam. He was blocking her out, shoving her away as forcefully as if it were physical. With silent steps, Susan made her way down the stairs.

"Adam, what's wrong?" she questioned softly.

His face twisted into a scowl. "Nothing."

"Obviously something's bothering you." She sat opposite him so that he couldn't avoid her.

"Have you ever thought about what a plain name Adam is?" he asked, and sighed heavily.

The faint odor of alcohol shocked Susan; she'd never known Adam to have more than one drink, two at the most. "Mine isn't exactly one of the more exotic ones," she offered, noting his impassive expression.

He ignored the comment, reaching instead for a stack of Silhouette romances on the table beside the chair. Opening one, he gave a short, humorless laugh. "Honestly, how many men do you know named Remington?"

"Well, there's that one on television," Susan returned.

Angrily he tossed the book aside and opened another. "How about Jefferson, Tate or Thornton?"

"What difference does it make what the names are?" Susan couldn't understand what was troubling him. If Adam was hurt and confused, she was doubly so.

"It makes one hell of a difference." Forcefully he expelled a harsh breath. Despair flickered across his face and he paused to run a hand over his eyes. "Have you taken a good look at the jackets of these books lately?"

"Of course I have. Silhouette's proud of the quality of their covers."

"They use real macho men for the models, don't they?"

"Some women think of them that way." Her voice faltered slightly. "Adam, I don't understand what any of this has to do with us."

"Susan, look at me. Look real good." His dark eyes probed hers. "They'd never use me on the cover of one of these books."

"Me neither! What does it matter?" Her eyes pleaded with him.

"You're on every one of them," he shouted. The back of his hand lashe out, knocking a stack of paperbacks onto the floor.

Susan gave a small gasp. "Adam! Won't you please tell me what's wrong!"

"There is no happy-ever-after, Susan," he murmured dejectedly. His brow was furrowed in a deep frown.

"You're not making any sense." She watched him with a sad, pleading expression.

The hard look in his eyes softened. "I know I'm not. Go up to bed and get some rest. We'll talk in the morning."

"I'm not going to sleep until this thing is cleared up. It's the fact that I'm a romance editor that disturbs you so much, isn't it?"

His eyes didn't leave hers. "I wish I'd known that from the beginning. It would have saved us both a lot of trouble."

"But why?" She almost shouted the question.

"Go upstairs. Please." He glanced away, refusing to bring his gaze to hers.

Talking wasn't doing any good. Whatever was troubling Adam had to be settled in his own mind. Bending, she reached down and straightened the books into a neat stack. "Good night, Adam."

"Good night," he mumbled. He looked at her sightlessly, his expression stoic.

Halfway up the stairs, Susan stopped to glance back on the dejected figure, yearning to answer his doubts and know his love, desperately afraid she never would.

Susan changed in and out of the three outfits so many times that her stomach had coiled into a tight ball. She'd hardly seen Adam all day. His mother had taken her out for some sight-seeing, but neither was really interested in what they were doing. Releasing a slow, painful breath, Susan decided to wear a fisherman knit sweater and tweed pants, knowing she looked lean and leggy. Her hair was styled softly on top of her head with short wisps framing her forehead and temples.

"Oh, Susan, you look lovely," Adam's mother said as she descended the stairs.

Adam stood and came forward to meet her. His mouth quirked derisively. "She always looks beautiful." The words weren't meant as a compliment, and Susan unconsciously winced at the pain that seared her heart.

They barely spoke as Adam drove them across Litchfield. As he brought her into the restaurant, he paused, glancing over the crowded room. Susan heard someone shout his name, and Adam gave an abrupt nod. Cupping her elbow, he led her into the dining room.

Susan couldn't remember being more nervous. Meeting Adam's mother had been less traumatic.

Adam made the introductions, and Susan shook hands with Lenny and his wife, Pam, who returned her smile. Next was Burt, a balding man with a prominent moustache, and his wife, Linda. Lastly Gary, the tall and good-looking attorney Susan had heard the most about, and his date, Michelle, a sleek blond. Space was cleared for them, and Lenny waved to the waitress, telling her they'd like to order cocktails.

Two rounds of drinks followed before Susan saw the menu. If anyone noticed that Adam was especially quiet, they didn't comment, nor did they attempt to draw Susan into the inconsequential chatter. When Gary tried to bring her into the conversation, she answered his questions with one-word responses and smiled, but the look didn't reach her eyes.

Their meal arrived and Susan did little more than sample the dinner. For all she was aware, the food might as well have been sawdust; everything she swallowed seemed to stick in her throat.

One look confirmed that Adam wasn't enjoying himself any more than she. When the dishes were cleared away, the small party moved into a cocktail lounge for an after-dinner drink. Although Susan was seated beside Adam, they could have been across the room from one another.

The evening was quickly becoming an ordeal, and Susan didn't know how much more of it she could take. When the band began playing, the other couples rose to their feet, leaving Susan and Adam alone. The air between them was heavy and thick, and Susan hung her head, pretending an inordinate interest in her drink.

When Adam reached across and took her hand, she brought her face up and met the weary look in his eyes.

"I've been acting like a pig all night," he said. "Why do you put up with me?"

For a second the words confirming her love nearly slipped from her mouth. "We all have an off day now and then," she told him softly. She wasn't looking for excuses. All Susan wanted was to have things right between them.

"Would you like to dance?" His invitation was issued on a husky murmur. He stood, offering her his hand.

Susan rolled back the chair and gracefully rose to her feet.

They'd never danced before, and she was amazed how perfectly they fit together, their steps matching one another's. For the first few minutes Adam held her stiffly, but gradually he relaxed, bringing her as close as possible. "Oh, Susan," he whispered in her ear. "You deserve so much better."

"That could be," she teased. Already the healing power of his touch soothed the pain of his earlier rejection. "But I only want you."

Groaning, he tightened his hold and gently kissed her temple.

When the band stopped playing, they came apart reluctantly and walked back to their table. Lenny came from behind and slapped Adam across the shoulders.

"You must be doing better than we thought," Adam's friend joked loudly. "Otherwise, what would a beauty like Susan be doing with you? Come on, good-looking, let's dance."

Before Susan could protest, she was jerked back onto the dance floor and into the eager man's arms.

Chapter Six

Shock and anger froze Susan until Lenny had reached the dance floor. When he skillfully twirled her into his arms, she made a small, protesting sound.

"You okay, little lady?"

"No," she murmured, but she felt like shouting at him. Lenny's unkind words could ruin everything. "How dare you say anything like that to Adam? How dare you?" She held herself unyielding and stiff against him.

The wide, friendly smile on Lenny's face relaxed. "No need to take offense. Adam knows I was teasing. Why, we've been friends since grade school. I know him better than you."

"I doubt that," she seethed. "I doubt that very much. Now if you don't mind, I'd rather sit this one out."

Lenny seemed relieved to be rid of her. Laughing, he grabbed his wife's arm and returned to the populated floor.

Adam's look was anxious. Susan noted how his eyes followed her as she weaved a path between the other dancers and around chairs.

"Lenny didn't try anything, did he?" Adam stood to meet her, and the question was issued in a deceptively calm voice. The hard set of Adam's mouth told her how angry he was.

"No." She shook her head, her eyes pleading with him. Giving him her hand in silent invitation, she whispered, "There's no one I want to dance with except you."

Adam hesitated before curving an arm around her waist and leading her back onto the floor. Automatically her arms went around his neck as she fit her body to his.

His fingers moved against the small of her back, molding her to him, arching her closer.

When he didn't say anything, Susan decided she must. "Are you angry?" She didn't need to clarify the question.

"No. Lenny only said what everyone's thinking."

"Oh, Adam," she moaned softly, "that's not true."

He squeezed her, his strong hands cutting deeply into her waist. "It's the most honest statement I've heard all night."

"Adam, Adam, Adam," she murmured, her voice weak and low. Gently she raised her head and kissed the harsh lines of his jaw. "Didn't your mother ever tell you beauty is in the eye of the beholder? And I behold you as my Prince Charming. Please don't let a few unkind words ruin our night. It got off to a shaky enough start as it is."

She could feel him smile against her temple and relaxed. Everything was going to be all right. Whatever had been bothering him had apparently been settled. Adam had answered the questions that troubled him.

Once Gary interrupted them, asking for a dance, but Adam laughed his friend off. "I'm not letting the prettiest girl here out of my arms. Find yourself another partner."

Gary looked surprised but agreed good-naturedly.

"You don't mind, do you?" Adam tipped his head back to watch her.

"I'd have minded a lot more if you'd let him take me."

Lifting her hand to his lips, Adam moved his mouth sensuously over the smooth skin of her palm. Susan felt her knees go weak at the potency of his touch.

"Two can play that game," she whispered, her teeth taking little nipping bites at his earlobe. Satisfaction came as she felt him shudder.

"Susan," he groaned, gathering her intimately close. "Let's get out of here."

"Okay," she agreed, shocked at how unnatural her voice sounded.

Adam's arms tightened around her. "Lord, I'm hungry. I don't know about you, but I didn't eat a bite of dinner."

"I nibble your earlobe and you start talking about food?" Susan sighed mockingly. "Where's the romance?"

Adam stiffened and nearly missed a step. "I'm not a romantic man," he returned in a tight voice.

Her hand caressed his angular jawline as she laid her head upon his chest. The ragged beat of his heart sounded in her ear. "I was only teasing," she whispered apologetically.

Capturing her hand, he kissed her fingers. "I know, I'm sorry."

"Now that you mention it," she said with a low laugh, "I am hungry."

"Ready to go?"

"More than ready."

They made their excuses and were out the door within ten minutes.

Two hours later Adam parked the station wagon in front of his mother's house. Coming around to her side, he opened the door and helped her out. Immediately he took her in his arms and kissed her hard and long, stealing her breath.

"What was that for?" Her feet still hadn't touched the ground. Even speaking coherently was difficult.

"My mother," he whispered, and chuckled. "She's staring out the upstairs window, and I wanted her to know everything's all right."

"So you kissed me for show, is that it?"

"That, and because I couldn't keep my hands off you another minute."

"Good, I didn't know if I could stand it much longer myself." Sliding her arms around his neck, she stood on the tips of her toes, her mouth teasing his with short kisses that promised more than satisfied.

"Susan," he groaned, "you're playing with fire."

"I know," she whispered seductively.

In response, Adam draped an arm over her shoulders and lead her toward the house. A light had been left on in the kitchen. Susan waited at the bottom of the stairs while Adam turned it off. Immediately the room was cast in darkness. The only light came from the flickering shadows of the moon as they played across the room.

Standing on the first stair, Susan waited for Adam to come to her. "Adam," she whispered, as he located her in the dark and slipped his arms around her waist. "Oh, Adam," she said softly.

He buried his face in her neck, holding her as if she was the most precious gift he would ever receive. Together they stood, neither speaking, in a world that seemed to be created for them, for this minute.

When his mouth found hers, Susan thought she'd die with longing. He didn't stop; he couldn't seem to get enough of her as his mouth lazily sought her eyes, her forehead, her cheeks and chin. Impatient fingers entwined with her hair, pulling out the pins that contained it. When it tumbled down like a thick brown curtain, he drew in a deep, shuddering breath and claimed her lips in a fierce, devouring kiss that left her weak and willing.

Susan could hear the wild, pounding beat of her heart echoing in her ears. She didn't protest when Adam coaxed her off the step and led her into the living room, lowering her onto the sofa. Her arms reached out to him as he brought her back into his embrace. Unerringly his mouth found hers, deepening the contact. His hands slid under the bulky sweater, caressing her back, slowly moving around to cup her full breasts. Intimately his thumb slid over the lacy outline until her nipples peaked and hardened.

"Susan, oh, Susan." An all-consuming fire had been ignited between them, but it wasn't right. Not here in his mother's home. Not now. She understood what he was saying without the words.

Weaving her fingers into the hair at the side of his head, she expelled a long, choppy breath and pulled him to her breast.

Adam held her for a long time, until his breathing was controlled and even. He helped her stand and loosely wrapped a hand around her waist to guide her up the stairs. Outside her bedroom door, he kissed her again. Lightly, sweetly, gently.

Susan didn't sleep for a long time afterward, knowing the only obstacles that separated her from Adam were two thin doors.

Olivia Gallagher hugged Susan as Adam slid the suitcases into the back end of the wagon. "Now don't make strangers of yourselves, you hear."

"We won't, Mother," Adam answered for both of them. Coming around to the side of the vehicle, he kissed his mother firmly on the cheek.

"Got the pie recipe?" Olivia quizzed, tucking a wisp of white hair back into place.

"Right here." Susan patted her purse. "I'll let you know how it turns out."

"Just remember to use Jonathan apples. That's the secret."

"I promise."

"Mother," Adam objected impatiently. "It's already three hours later than I'd planned on heading out."

Giving them each another quick kiss, Olivia stepped back and Adam helped Susan inside. He came around and started the engine. After a quick wave they were off.

The day had been beautiful. Church in the morning and then an early Thanksgiving dinner with Adam's sister, Theresa, and her family afterward. Adam had said something that morning about making it back to New York before dark. But already dusk was beginning to set.

Susan settled back comfortably and almost instantly fell asleep. Adam woke her outside her apartment.

"We're back already?" Susan asked on a yawn as she sat up and stretched, raising her arms high above her head.

Inserting her key into the apartment lock, Susan pushed open the door and stopped abruptly. Something was wrong. She couldn't immediately say what it was, but something was definitely different.

"What's the matter?" Adam asked from behind her."

"I don't know. Rosemary," she called out softly. Hurried strides carried her across the small apartment to the lone bedroom. Opening the door, Susan stopped and gasped.

"She's gone," she cried, trying to keep the panic out of her voice.

"Who's gone?"

"Rosemary," she shouted unreasonably. "All her things are missing. That's what's different. Rosemary's gone." Her voice wobbled uncontrollably. "Someone kidnapped my roommate. Oh, Adam, what can I do?"

Running a hand over his face, he stood, his brow wrinkled in thick lines. "It's unlikely that a kidnapper would move her things."

A noise outside the apartment drew their attention. With a smile of happiness, Rosemary floated into the apartment.

"Rosemary," Susan cried, returning to the living room. "What's going on?"

Susan's roommate all but danced across the floor. "I got married." Proudly she held out her hand. The ring finger sparkled with a tiny diamond.

"Carl?" Susan asked in disbelief.

"Not Carl, silly. Fred."

"Fred," Susan gasped, and slowly lowered herself onto the couch. "Who's Fred?"

"The guy from the health-food store. You know Fred."

"Oh, that Fred."

"Will someone please tell me what's going on here?" Adam inquired in measured tones.

Susan ignored him. "Isn't this rather sudden?"

"You know me," Rosemary answered, laughing off her friend's concern. "Once I make up my mind about something, I don't like to sit on it. Fred felt the same way. Aren't you going to congratulate me?"

"You idiot," Susan said, and sniffled. "You crazy fool, I'm going to miss you terribly."

"I know." Rosemary laughed gaily. "I thought about that for a long time, but our tiny bedroom simply isn't big enough for the three of us."

It felt strange to live alone, but Susan decided not to get another roommate. That meant a tight budget and watching her pennies, but she knew she could manage it.

Monday morning Susan was at the park expecting to meet Adam for their usual run. When he didn't show up, Susan assumed he was extra busy or had forgotten. When he wasn't there Tuesday or Wednesday, she felt hurt and disappointed. Was he playing games with her again? He'd given her more trouble than any ten men she had dated previously. Well, she could play some games of her own. For the rest of the week she didn't bother to go to the park. But when the weekend arrived, she couldn't stand it any longer.

Against her better judgment, against everything she wanted to prove in this relationship, she called him.

The phone rang five times before he answered. "Yes," he snapped.

"It's Susan." Her resolve nearly wavered with the unwelcome note in his voice.

The pause was almost indiscernible, but enough for her to notice. "I've been meaning to phone. I've had a hectic week." His voice softened somewhat.

"I thought you probably had."

Silence.

"You're closing me out again, aren't you?"

"No." He was lying and they both knew it. "I've just been busy, that's all."

"Too busy to run? You love to jog."

"Maybe next week. Listen, Susan, I'd like to chat but I've got something going on here. I'll give you a call next week."

"Sure," she whispered through the hurt. "Sure, Adam, I'll talk to you later."

True to his word, he did phone the following week, but the conversation was short and stilted. More than once Susan had to bite her tongue to keep from screaming at him. She was certain he'd given up running because he didn't want to meet her. Before they hung up, she told him that her schedule had been changed and she wasn't going to be able to jog anymore. It was a half-truth, but she didn't want to deprive him of something he enjoyed. Although Adam didn't comment, Susan felt confident he knew what she was saying.

Another week passed without hearing from him. Whatever was troubling Adam had to be settled in his own way. Susan didn't know what more she could do. Adam couldn't hold her and kiss her as he had, then turn away so abruptly. Obviously there were problems he needed to work out. And she had her pride, too. In the past she had been the one to pursue him. Perhaps if she backed off and gave Adam breathing room, he could settle this within himself. When he was ready, she'd be waiting.

Because she was lonely, Susan began dating again. No one special and never the same man for more than a few times. Casual dates with friends. She threw herself into her work, often staying until six or seven so that she'd be so tired she wouldn't stop to answer the nagging doubts. Or give in to the impulse to contact him.

Adam continued to phone, usually when she least

expected it. He didn't ask her out again, or suggest that they meet, and Susan didn't prod.

At Christmas she spent hours searching for a special card that would say exactly how she felt, deciding in the end that she'd never find one. She ended up mailing the same one that she had sent to all her family and friends.

Adam mailed her a card with his name scribbled at the bottom. There was no written message. Susan wondered if he had searched for the perfect card as she had. She doubted it.

A few days before Christmas he phoned. Again when she had least expected him to call—early on a Saturday morning.

"Hello, Susan, I'm not interrupting anything, am I?"

"No, of course not." Didn't he know by now that he was the most important person in her life?

"I just wanted to wish you a Merry Christmas."

"You too, Adam." She paused and an awkward silence followed.

"Are you going home for the holidays?"

"Yes, I'm flying out the twenty-third and will be back the twenty-sixth." She couldn't afford it, but her parents had paid part of the air fare. Susan was sure her mother knew something was wrong, although Susan hadn't written anything about Adam or their relationship. She wondered what her family would think if she confessed she was in love with a man who didn't love her. Probably disbelief.

"You're not staying long, are you?" It was more a statement than a question.

"I can't spare the time from the office."

Another silence.

"Are you driving to your mother's?" Susan asked.

"Yes. She sent her love, by the way." His mother's love, but not his.

"Tell her Merry Christmas for me. Theresa and her family too."

"I will." He hesitated. "Well, I suppose I should be going. I didn't want to disturb you."

"You're not."

"Are you jogging these days?"

"All the time," she lied cheerfully, anything to keep the conversation going. She didn't want to hang up, not when she hadn't talked to him in days. "I . . . was thinking about going this morning, in fact."

"I won't keep you then. Good-bye, Susan, have a nice holiday."

For a long time after the line was disconnected, she held on to the receiver. She hadn't seen him since before Thanksgiving and was starving for the sight of him. Maybe he'd been hinting that he'd be at the park. Even the slightest possibility of running into him was enough for her to dig through her drawers and pull out the turquoise sweatsuit she had once treasured so highly.

Shivering, Susan briskly walked the two-and-a-half-mile course, desperately clinging to the hope of seeing Adam. When he hadn't shown by the time she'd finished the full circle, tears of frustration and disappointment filled her eyes. Tilting her head back, she took in huge breaths to quell their flow. She sat down on a bench where she used to meet Adam in the mornings. Sniffling, she stood, knowing how silly she must look walking around Central Park at Christmas time with tears in her eyes. Her throat hurt with the effort of suppressing the flow.

What was the matter with her? Was she so obtuse that she didn't understand that Adam didn't want to see her again? Hadn't he made himself crystal clear? For whatever his reasons, she mused, to ignore her or not to ignore her was his prerogative.

Was she so weak that her ego couldn't withstand the rejection? Maybe if she didn't love him so much, it would have been easier. This was just the kind of thing her authors weaved novels about. Wasn't it Adam who had told her: "There is no happy-ever-after." The time had come for her to accept that.

A chilly breeze caused her to shiver. A tear escaped and made a wet track down her pale face. Quickly she wiped it aside and pressed an index finger under each eye to stop others from escaping.

Dejected, defeated, discouraged, she returned to her apartment and took a warm bath.

"Karen would like to see you in her office," the receptionist, Dana Milton, told Susan when she walked into the office the second Monday in January. Christmas with her family had been wonderful. Wrapped securely in their love, Susan had returned to New York feeling relaxed and refreshed.

Stopping off at her small office, Susan hung up her coat and placed her purse in the bottom drawer of her desk. The telephone was already ringing, but Susan ignored it. On her way past the receptionist, she asked Dana to hold all her calls.

In the last part of the month she was scheduled to fly to Texas and speak at a writers' conference. She liked to travel and get the opportunity to meet authors. The conference was probably what Karen wanted to talk to her about.

It wasn't. The first thing that came into her mind as she went back to her office was that she'd need to have new business cards printed. How silly her thoughts had come to be lately. She was now a full editor and no longer an associate.

The first person she called was Adam. She'd never phoned his office, and hadn't talked to him since before Christmas.

"Dr. Gallagher's office." His receptionist sounded young and pretty and Susan immediately fought back the hot waves of jealousy.

"Hello," the voice repeated.

"I'm sorry." Susan breathed in sharply. "This is Susan Mackenzie. Would it be possible to speak with Dr. Gallagher?"

"I'm sorry, Dr. Gallagher's with a patient."

"Please tell him it's me, I'll hold."

She didn't know if he'd come to the phone or not. An inordinate amount of time seemed to pass before the receptionist came back on the line.

"He'll be right with you."

"Thank you." Susan sighed gratefully.

Not more than a minute later and the phone was connected again. "Susan, are you all right?"

"Yes, I'm sorry. I know I shouldn't call you like this, but I had some news. Some good news," she amended, "and you were the first person I wanted to tell. I got a promotion. I'm a full-fledged editor now."

"Congratulations. I'm sure you deserve it." The genuine pleasure in his voice created a warm glow within her.

"At least it means I'll be able to keep the apartment. Although I hate to see the entire amount of my raise go toward the rent, I've discovered I like living alone. I don't think I could find anyone else who'd put up with me the way Rosemary did."

His chuckle was warm and friendly. "I'm very pleased for you, Susan." It was the most they'd said to one another in weeks.

"I won't keep you. I know this is an awful time to phone, but I was so excited I wanted to tell someone."

"I'm glad you did." He didn't tell her he'd talk to her soon, or again, or anything. But she didn't notice it at the time, only later. Much later.

An hour after their conversation, a dozen red roses were delivered to her office. Beautiful roses. The sender's card bore only one word: "Adam."

With the promotion came new responsibilities, and Susan threw herself into the task eagerly. Not until another week had passed did Susan realize she hadn't heard from Adam. Nothing since before Christmas. Only the roses. Had he given up phoning her too?

Five days later, Susan nervously dialed his phone number. Her hand shook as she lifted the receiver to her ear. Nothing had ever seemed more difficult.

He answered on the third ring. "Hello."

"Hello, Adam, I haven't heard from you in a long

time." She forced a cheerful note into her voice, aware she wasn't fooling him. "Did you get my card?"

"It arrived last week. There wasn't any need to thank me."

"Of course there was," she contradicted softly. "The reason I phoned was to let you know there's going to be a small party celebrating my promotion at Rosemary and Fred's next Friday night."

He hesitated, and the taut silence vibrated in her ears. "I'll have to check my calendar."

"Go ahead, I can wait." If he declined, Susan didn't know how she'd react.

He didn't take more than a few minutes. "It looks like I've got hospital duty that night."

Disappointment washed over her. "I'll talk to Rosemary. I'm sure we can change the party to Saturday night without too much trouble."

She heard the irritation in his short sigh. "I don't want you to do that."

"But I'd like you to be there. I haven't seen you in months."

"I told you, I'm busy," he said gruffly.

"Adam." She forced herself not to plead. "This is important to me."

"You know the way I feel about parties."

Her laugh was short and derisive. "We met at a party! Are you saying that you'd accept an invitation from Ralph Jordan, but not from me?"

The line seemed to crackle with the tense silence. "I told you, I'm busy."

"Adam," she pleaded, angry with herself. "Please."

"Susan, *no.*"

Never had any word sounded more hurtful or cruel. For a moment she closed her eyes as the pain of this final rejection seared her heart.

"I won't trouble you again," she whispered achingly, hating herself for the way her voice wavered.

"Good-bye, Susan." His voice had softened slightly, and she realized it wasn't her imagination when she heard the painful regret.

The next day Susan met Rosemary for lunch at a small deli in Rockefeller Center. Susan forced down soup and a sandwich, and Rosemary dug into a yogurt thick with nuts and fruit.

"Would you mind very much if we canceled the idea of a big party?" Susan asked casually. "Parties can be such a hassle, and I think I'd like it more if we all went to dinner at that new vegetarian restaurant you've been telling me about." Susan hoped her friends would forgive her.

"Great idea," Rosemary agreed instantly. "I'll make the arrangements and get back to you later."

"You don't need to do anything, you know that."

"Are you kidding," Rosemary teased. "Fred and I are looking for an event to announce that I'm pregnant."

Susan stopped eating, the sandwich lifted halfway to her mouth. "Rosemary," she whispered, her eyes round and happy, "that's wonderful."

"I know. Fred and I are really pleased. I wanted Adam to be my doctor. He understands my desire for proper diet. You don't mind, do you?"

"Of course not. Have you seen him yet?"

"Two days ago. He asked about you."

Susan hid her surprise; but then, it was only natural that he would make a polite inquiry. She didn't fool herself by making more out of it. That's all it was.

Thinking about her conversation with Rosemary later, Susan mentally marked February first on the calendar. That should be enough time for Adam to have sorted through his feelings. He might want her to believe he didn't love or need her, but she knew him too well. Adam Gallagher wasn't the kind of man who could hold her in his arms one day and be hurtful the next.

Setting a date in her mind served another purpose. It gave Susan a day to set her sights on, a day to hope for. If he hadn't contacted her by then, the solution was simple. She'd go to him. Turning her away would be far more difficult if he had to look her in the eyes.

The morning of February second she made an appointment with his receptionist. A few days later she sat nervously in one of his examination rooms, her teeth nibbling on the soft flesh of her lip. Several times she clenched and unclenched her fists. She prayed this was the right thing to do. Once again she was swallowing her pride and coming to him.

"Susan?" The disapproval in his voice did little to calm her. But when he glanced up from the chart, a gleam softened the hard look in his eyes. "You've cut your hair."

She'd forgotten he hadn't seen it. Her hand fingered the shoulder-length curls. "It's not as short as it looks. I had it styled is all. Do you like it?"

He ignored the question. "What's the problem?" He

made no move to examine her, instead he leaned against a chair on the opposite side of the room as if he wished to put as much distance between them as possible in the cramped quarters.

"Don't look so welcoming," she said with forced gaiety. "Don't you remember you said I could come see you if I was sick."

"I remember." He didn't look pleased about it.

"I'm having a small pain," she continued, undaunted.

"Where?"

"On the left side of my chest, about the center."

"Your heart?" he questioned sarcastically.

Susan smiled weakly. Her idea hadn't been that creative.

"Let me listen," he returned crisply, and walked to the table where she was perched. Lifting up the back of her sweater, he placed the cold stethoscope on her sensitive flesh. "Take deep breaths."

Susan complied, drawing in several mouthfuls of air. This wasn't going well. What had she expected? It was all she could do not to reach out to him, touch him. The minute he'd walked into the room, she'd drunk in the virile sight of him. He looked tired, as if he was putting in long hours, but then so was she—immersing herself in work to forget.

"Everything sounds fine," he said flatly. His mouth moved into a forbidding line as he moved to the small desk and pulled out a pad.

"Adam," she whispered entreatingly. "I've waited three months to see you. At first you phoned me, now you don't even do that. Almost three months, Adam. I thought by this time you would have worked things out. I need you. I'm miserable."

He ripped the sheet from the pad and stood handing it to her. "Have your druggist fill this."

"Are you listening to me at all?" She raised her voice, pleading with him.

His eyes refused to meet hers. "If you continue to have problems, I'd suggest you see a specialist. My practice is limited and I doubt that I'll be able to help you." His hand clenched the doorknob, and Susan noted that although his voice was cool and detached, his knuckles were white.

"Don't do this to us, please." She hung her head, the soft curls falling forward to shield her from the final embarrassment.

"That prescription should take care of any problems you have. Good-bye, Susan."

She didn't even bother to read it, knowing it was for placebos. Dejected, she stood and put on her coat. Grabbing her purse, she hurried out of the office. Not until she was seated in the taxi did Susan decide that this is what it must feel like to die. Her stomach was constricting into a tight ball of pain. Swallowing, breathing, talking were almost impossible.

The cab jerked in and out of traffic, speeding up only to have the driver slam on his brakes a minute later. Susan hardly noticed. Every New York cabdriver she'd ever ridden with drove in the same way.

Not until he yelled at her to hold on did Susan look

up and see a bus racing out of control, heading directly for the passenger side of the cab. Only then did she let out a scream.

The terror in her own voice was the only thing she heard as metal slammed against metal and she was violently thrown against the door.

Chapter Seven

Deep, piercing pain filtered into the dark world in which Susan lay. Her head throbbed so hard and strong that she raised a tentative hand to feel what could be hurting so badly. Her fingers encountered a gauze wrapping. She tried to open her eyes, but they felt weighted as if someone were pressing to keep them shut. One refused to open; the other opened just enough for her to recognize that the bright overhead lights must be in a hospital.

A raised voice could be heard coming from the other side of the room. "I want a plastic surgeon brought in."

"I don't think she'll need—"

The first voice didn't get the chance to finish.

"I don't care what you think, I want one and I want one now. Is that understood?" His irritation seemed to vibrate across the room.

"Yes, doctor."

Adam. Adam's voice was the angry one. Susan had never heard him talk that way to anyone.

From the distance came the sound of soft moaning. Not until Adam moved to her side did Susan realize the groans were her own.

"So you're awake." The gentle quality she loved about him was back. "We were beginning to wonder how much longer you'd be out. How do you feel?"

For a moment her mouth refused to obey, and when she finally managed to speak, the words felt thick and heavy. "Don't ask."

"I'll have the nurse give you something for the pain."

She tried to reach out and touch him, but his hand stopped hers, gripping her fingers. Slowly his thumb caressed the back of her wrist in a gentle, soothing movement.

"You've been in an accident," he explained in a soft, assuring tone. "The reason you can't open one eye is because it's swollen shut. The pain in your chest is from cracked ribs."

"My head?"

"I imagine it feels like it's split wide open. You've got a whopper of a concussion."

Even with only one eye opened just enough to see, Susan noted the twitch of a nerve in his hand, lean jaw as he looked down at her. Hadn't she heard him demanding that a plastic surgeon be called?

"My face?" Her voice quivered. What had happened to her that made Adam look at her like that?

"Luckily you put your hands up, which prevented

your face from being cut anymore than it was. There are several scratches. Nothing major."

A weariness flooded her, waves of fatigue rippling through her. Susan fought it as long as she could. Finally she succumbed to the overwhelming force as Adam whispered something about talking to her later.

When she woke again there were no bright lights overhead. The railing on the bed assured her she was still in the hospital. Her mind buzzed with questions. Why had Adam been in the emergency room? How had he known about the accident?

Her mouth felt thick, as if someone had stuffed it with cotton. She longed for a taste of cool water. Maybe she could ring the nurse. Although her hand fumbled around the bedside for a buzzer, she couldn't find one and eventually fell back to sleep.

The room was filled with light when Susan was stirred awake. She turned her head when a tall nurse opened the door and stepped into the room.

"Morning, I thought you'd be awake by now." The white-capped nurse moved to the side of the bed and stuck a thermometer in Susan's mouth. Fascinated, Susan watched as the digital readout showed her exact temperature. The nurse discarded the mouthpiece and checked the bottle and tubes connecting the I.V. in Susan's arm.

"When will Dr. Gallagher be in?" Susan questioned, following the woman's actions as the efficient nurse progressed around the bed.

"Dr. Gallagher?" she repeated. A frown marred her wide forehead as she removed the chart clipped at the end of the bed. "You've been assigned to Dr. Manson."

"But Dr. Gallagher saw me in the emergency room; I'm sure he did." It hadn't been her imagination. She was positive Adam had been there.

"Dr. Gallagher examined you when you were admitted, but your chart shows Dr. Manson's name. You can ask about it later when Dr. Manson does his rounds."

Susan didn't need to ask, she already knew. Adam had requested to be relieved of her case. It shouldn't have surprised her, but it did—almost as much as it hurt. When he'd rejected her so many times, how could she hope to believe he'd care now?

"Would you like something to drink?" the kind woman offered.

"Please," she mumbled. "And would it be possible, I mean . . . could I see a mirror?"

"There's one above the sink, but for right now I'm sure Dr. Manson would like you to stay in bed. I don't think we have a hand mirror available. If you'd like, I could ask."

"What do I look like?" Susan knew it was an unfair question, but she had to know.

"Let's put it this way," the nurse chuckled. "I wouldn't want to see the other guy. But you'll improve. Don't worry."

Dr. Manson was a short man with thinning gray hair and twinkling blue eyes. Susan liked him immediately.

"Good morning."

She offered him a weak smile. "Morning. When can I go home?" All she wanted to do was get out of there.

"Soon," he said, and laughed. "I swear, some people don't know when they've got it good. You're the third person this morning who would prefer other accommodations." Lifting her chart from the end of the bed, he skimmed over its contents and shook his head approvingly. "We were worried last night about internal injuries, but you seem to be doing fine. I imagine tomorrow we can release you if you like."

"I like," she stated emphatically.

"Don't do too much today. Get out of bed if you want. I've got you on a soft-food diet, and I'll check with you tomorrow morning."

"Thank you, doctor."

Breakfast arrived and Susan looked at it disparagingly. She managed to down the mushy applesauce and a small bowl of Jell-O. Afterward she was so weak she lay back and, before she knew it, was sound asleep.

A noise in the room woke her. When she opened her eyes, Adam was standing beside her bed.

"Shouldn't you be in your office?" she asked, surprised at how distant her voice sounded.

"I just finished delivering a baby and thought I'd check and see how you're doing."

Turning her head, she purposely looked away from him. "Fine," she mumbled.

"Dr. Manson says you'll be able to go home tomorrow. I'll take half the day off and pick you up about noon."

Susan jerked her head around, shocked at his offer, then winced at the pain that shot through her head. Hadn't he made it clear that he didn't want to see her again? What had altered his decision? Obviously the

change of heart had been a sudden one. Only a few
hours ago he had given her case to another doctor.
Having her as a patient was more than he was willing to
do.

Pride nearly erected its vindictive head as she began
to insist she didn't need him, could find her own way
home. But something stopped her. It didn't take her
long to recognize that she was willing to accept the
crumbs he offered. She didn't care what the reason was
as long as Adam was there.

"You were in the emergency room last night, weren't
you?"

Adam agreed with a blunt shake of his head. "They
called me."

"But how? I didn't give anyone your name."

He glanced away, an uneasy look flickering across his
face. "Apparently the prescription I gave you was
clenched in your fist. The ambulance driver found it."

"Adam," she whispered imploringly. "Is my face
bad? No one wants to tell me anything."

Again she noted how a nerve twitched in his jaw, but
his eyes softened. "You've got a few cuts, but they'll
heal quickly. Your eye's swollen, but quite a bit less
than yesterday." He hesitated. "You're still the most
beautiful woman I know."

"Oh, Adam." She sniffled as turbulent emotions
engulfed her, nearly overtaking the delicate hold she
had on her composure. To hide her reaction, she asked
another question. "Do you know anything about the
cabdriver? Was he hurt?"

"Cuts and bruises. From what I understand he was
treated at the scene and released." He paused, and a

finger lovingly traced her lips. "You really are beautiful."

His hand squeezed hers and she felt the moisture build in her eyes. Wiping a tear away, she tried to laugh. "Look at me. You tell me I'm pretty and I cry."

"I'm not going to convince you everything's fine until you've seen for yourself. Here, sit up." He reached behind her to the bed controller, pushing the button that folded the bed upright. "There's only a few scrapes and bruises, trust me."

Once he'd positioned the bed so that she was sitting upright, he opened the small closet beside the sink and took out her housecoat and slippers.

"How'd you get those?" She stared incredulously at her velvet robe and matching slippers.

Adam's look was almost boyish. "Yes . . . well, I took the liberty of opening your purse and taking out the key to your apartment. I brought some other things I thought you might need. You don't mind, do you?"

"No, of course not." Would this man ever stop amazing her?

"I also contacted the Silhouette offices and told them about the accident. Rosemary phoned me later and I assured her you were going to be fine. She said to tell you she'll be in later today. You're not to worry about a thing, everything's been taken care of."

Folding the covers back, Adam helped her to scoot her legs over the edge of the bed. Bending down on one knee, he placed her slippers on her feet, then helped her slip her arms into the robe.

"What about the I.V.?" Susan looked up anxiously.

"Not to worry," he assured her, and wheeled the tall

pole with the attached plastic bottle to the side of the bed.

"What is this stuff anyway?" She eyed the whole setup suspiciously.

"Sugar water with some antibiotics to ward off infection," he told her. Offering his hand, he smiled encouragingly. "You ready?"

"As I'll ever be." A small stool rested beside the bed, and Susan tentatively placed a foot on the grooved black surface. The hospital gown rode up to expose the top of her thigh and she moved quickly, then sucked in her breath at the sharp pain that pierced her ribs.

Adam wrapped an arm around her waist. "Hey, not so fast."

Guiding her with a protective hand, he led her to the mirror. One glimpse of her cut, ravaged face and she let out a gasp of dismay. Her left eye was grotesquely swollen, and deep purple color covered one side of her upper face extending as far down as her cheekbone. Tiny cuts and scrapes outlined the delicate curve of her jaw. White gauze was wrapped around her head, and she noted two butterfly bandages near her hairline.

"It's beauty and the beast all right," she whispered brokenly. "Only I'm the beast." A huge lump quickly formed in her throat as she buried her face in Adam's chest.

"It's not so bad," he whispered soothingly. "Within a month no one will know you were ever hurt."

"A month," she groaned.

"Honey, believe me, when I first saw you, I was afraid it was much worse."

Honey! The affectionate term rolled off his tongue as

if he'd said it a thousand times. A silly weakness seemed to attack her legs and she swayed toward him.

Quickly Adam's arm held her secure. "Let's get you back into bed. Rest today. I'll be back tonight to help you walk."

"Yes, doctor," she retorted primly.

A crooked smile slanted across his mouth. His lips lightly brushed her cheek as he helped her back to bed.

"I'll see you later," he promised.

Susan leaned against the pillow and sighed. Immediately her ribs protested, and she released a quivering breath until the pain subsided.

Rosemary stuck her head in the door at lunchtime. "Susan," she cried, unable to hide her shock. "Oh my goodness."

"I know, it's awful, isn't it?"

Her friend moved tentatively into the room. "Here, Fred and I wanted you to have this." She set a bushy plant on the table beside the bed. "It's an aloe vera plant. They're wonderful for all sorts of medicinal purposes. I brought along a booklet for you to read . . . only you probably shouldn't with that eye. At least not right away."

"Thanks, Rosie. I'll keep it in the medicine cabinet."

"Now I know you're going to be all right," Rosemary said, and gave an approvingly look. "When you can tease, then you must almost be back to normal." She walked to the window. "Not a bad view."

"Honestly, for what this room's costing me, I could be vacationing on the Mediterranean."

Rosemary agreed and glanced at her watch. "I gotta

get back to the salt mines. Are you sure there isn't anything I can do for you?"

"Smuggle me in a pastrami on rye and hold the mayo," she shot back hopefully.

"Are you nuts!" Rosemary's round eyes widened with disbelief. "You're asking the wrong person. Adam would have my head. Do you have any idea how bad pastrami is for you?"

A flick of Susan's wrist dismissed the advice. "I don't want to know. All I care about is something that doesn't swim in my mouth when I swallow."

"Tofu on—," Rosemary offered sincerely.

"Forget it, Rosie, I'll eat cherry flavored gelatin."

"The hospital is filling you with that junk!" Bright brown eyes burned with outrage. "Boy, they better not try it when I'm here." Patting the slight swell of her tummy, she gave a determined look. "Baby and I are only interested in good food."

"I'm sure Adam will make the proper arrangements," Susan assured her, silently questioning Rosemary's definition of good food.

The indignation dissipated. "If you need anything, let me know. Okay?"

"I will." She smiled softly. "Thanks for coming." Her head had begun to throb again and her ribs ached. Settling back, she flipped the switch to the television and ran through a variety of stations. Finding nothing to interest her, she took another nap.

After dinner Adam returned, helping her out of bed and walking at her side as they strolled the hallway several times. One hand was linked with Adam's while the other pushed the portable I.V. pole. Two beautiful floral bouquets had arrived that afternoon. One was from Adam and another from her co-workers at Silhouette. Adam didn't look at either one, nor at the plant Rosemary had brought. The thought passed through Susan's mind that he didn't want to know if another man had sent her flowers. For a time she tried to think of a natural way to assure him that he was the only one, but she abandoned the idea because he would know exactly what she was doing.

"How long will it be before I can go back to work?" she quizzed as they made their last round and headed back to her room.

"I think a week should do it."

"A week," she cried, her voice high with consternation. "I can't miss that much time." Already her mind was racing toward a writers' conference she was scheduled to speak at in Florida in the middle of March."

"Sure you can," he contradicted.

"But, Adam," she continued the protest, "I'll go crazy sitting in that apartment every day all by myself."

"After the first couple of days, I don't see why you couldn't go in for a few hours in the mornings. But not any more than that," he warned.

Susan lay for a long time thinking after Adam had kissed her good night. A light kiss against her forehead. Just the day before, he had forcefully pushed her from his life. The accident was the only reason he was back. But for how long? Should she prepare herself for another separation? She had never been this close to a man, this vulnerable. The power he had to hurt her was beyond even her own understanding. Caring this deeply for someone had called for risks, and she had been the one to step forward. Not Adam. Just when she was sure she'd lost him forever, he was back. That frightened her more than losing him.

Adam stopped in briefly early the next morning with the reminder that she should be ready to leave about noon. Later, when Susan checked the closet, she found a set of loose-fitting clothes and marveled at how Adam seemed to think of everything.

Dr. Manson gave his smiling approval when he checked on her shortly after Adam left. He stood chatting with her for several minutes after completing a thorough examination and signing the release papers. "So, you're Adam Gallagher's girl. I must admit I've never seen him lose his cool the way he did after they brought you into the emergency room."

At Susan's shocked look, Manson continued. "Most doctors agree it's better not to treat family members, or those we love. The difficulty is in keeping ourselves detached enough not to react emotionally. It only took me two seconds to see Adam cared deeply for you."

Susan wanted to argue that she was sure he was mistaken. But was he? Did Adam truly love her? If so, what could have prompted him to act as he had these last months? One thing she did know—she couldn't take any more hurt and rejection. Adam was back; she didn't question why or for how long. Gladly she accepted what he offered. But when he chose to leave, and Susan was sure he would, then she would allow him to go freely. For three miserable months she'd hung on to the hope, the dream of his love. But no more.

As he'd promised, Adam sauntered into her room at noon, pushing a wheelchair as though it were a grocery cart. He twirled it around a couple of times, making her smile.

"Show off," she admonished gently.

A hand under her elbow helped her off the bed. "Ready?"

"Am I ever! Does everyone feel this way?"

"What way?"

"Eager to get home. Everyone's been wonderful, and even the food, what there was of it, wasn't half-bad. But I'm so ready to go home."

"Almost everyone," he assured her. Slowly he lowered his gaze to the rapid pulse hammering at the base of her throat. Mentally Susan chastised herself for not having more control over her response. One slow, appraising look and she crumpled at his feet. His dark eyes roamed her face, the sensual tension building until her stomach tightened. Angrily she jerked her head aside. What was the use? She was only setting herself up for more hurt.

During the ride home, Adam worked hard to lighten the mood and tear down the tension between them. Joking, he carried her things into the apartment, set her on the sofa, and fluffed up the pillows.

Susan tried her hardest to throw herself into his happy mood but failed miserably. When Adam insisted on cooking their dinner, she watched with amazement as he set the table and brought out an expensive bottle of wine.

As much as Susan wanted and needed him, she

couldn't let this continue. She knew his motives. "Adam," she whispered, "the accident wasn't your fault."

His high spirits were lost as he expelled his breath forcefully. "I know that."

"Then why are you doing this? I don't know how to react when you're kind to me. I'm afraid." To her horror, large tears filled her eyes and spilled down her colorless cheeks.

Adam ripped the apron from his waist in one angry movement and tossed it across the room. "Damn it, Susan. Don't cry. I can't stand to see you cry."

"Then just leave." Her voice wobbled ridiculously as she pointed a finger at the front door.

Frozen, Adam stared back at her as if a tug-of-war were pulling him from both sides. Finally he reacted, grabbing his jacket from the back of the chair.

"Don't you dare leave me," she shouted, and hiccuped ingloriously.

He got as far as the front door, his hand on the knob. His back was to her and she watched as a shudder went through him.

"I need you," she whispered, her voice so low it was almost inaudible. She wasn't referring to the accident, and they both knew it.

When he turned, a tumult of emotions played over his strong face. Pride, indecision, pain and something she couldn't recognize.

Of its own volition, her hand reached out to him. The action seemed to break something within him and he hurried to her side, falling to his knees and wrapping his arms around her. Even in his urgency he was conscious of her ribs and the pain his hold could inflict.

"Susan, dear God." He murmured her name over and over again, rubbing his chin against her hair. "I saw you in that room, blood everywhere, and I died a thousand deaths. If I lost you . . ." He didn't finish.

Her hands roamed his back, loving the feel of him as she buried her face in the wide expanse of his chest. "Oh, Adam," she cried, tears streaming down her face. "I've missed you so much. You sent me away and I wanted to die."

Gently he broke the contact. His large hands framed her face as he lovingly spread kisses over her lips and cheeks and forehead, as if to kiss away the pain of his rejection.

"Adam." His name slipped from her lips in a half-pleading cry.

A tense groan was muffled as he found her mouth and savored again and again the softness of her lips.

Her hand left his shoulder and lovingly explored the line of his jaw before curving into the thick dark hair. The kiss hardened, demanding and relentless, drawing from Susan her heart, and touching the softness of her soul.

When he pulled away, his breathing was hoarse and uneven. "Susan, we've got to stop," he groaned.

"I know," she agreed, and unbuttoned his shirt, desperate for the feel of his bare skin. When her fingers encountered the cloud of dark hair, Susan became incapable of coherent thought. Right or wrong, she hadn't the power to reason anymore. The potent masculine feel of him enveloped her senses until they cried out at fever pitch.

When Adam's hands opened her blouse and cupped her unrestrained breasts, he gently kneaded their fullness and she grew weak with desire. Lost in a mindless whirlpool, Susan groaned softly, encouragingly, as his head bent to kiss the swelling curve.

He pressed her back against the couch, and Susan drew in a sharp breath as pain pierced her ribs.

Adam hesitated, then pulled away. Still within the circle of his embrace, she could feel his aching regret.

"I'm sorry, love," he whispered in a quivering breath.

"Sorry?" she repeated. A shudder wracked her shoulders, and Adam kissed her softly as if the action would absorb her pain.

His mouth twisted wryly as he lifted his head. "Those ribs must be hurting like hell," he muttered thickly.

"Not as much as . . ." She paused, biting off the words. He already knew how much sending her away had hurt. At the time, Susan hadn't been aware of how acutely he'd shared that pain.

"Are you ready for a glass of wine?" His jaw was set in a determined line as he battled his need and desire. Gently he tugged her arms from his neck. He kissed her fingertips and then the bridge of her nose before helping her fasten her blouse. She hadn't worn a bra intentionally. The restraining fabric would have cut into her ribs, hurting the tender area.

"I . . . I didn't know you had a hairy chest." Her voice was incredibly weak.

"You never asked." His voice didn't sound any less affected. Standing, he moved into the kitchen and returned with two glasses of wine, handing her one.

"Do you always keep dead flowers?" he quizzed, sitting opposite her.

Susan smiled softly to herself, aware that he had purposely taken a seat across from her so as not to be tempted. "Dead what?"

"Looks like roses, or what used to be roses." He picked a long stem from the vase resting beside the chair on the end table.

"Oh, those. I didn't have the heart to throw them out."

A coldness frosted his eyes as he lifted the wineglass to his lips and took a drink. "Someone special must have given them to you, for you to keep them this long," he commented with light pretense as his eyes avoided hers.

"Someone very special did," she returned.

"Who?" His voice was rough in demand. Vaulting to his feet, he stalked to the other side of the room. "No, don't answer that. I don't have any right to know."

"The next time you send a lady roses, the least you can do is remember it."

"Me?" He swiveled around sharply, a shocked look on his face. "When?"

"You honestly don't remember?" she teased. It was obvious he didn't. "When I was promoted."

Wearily, Adam slouched back into the chair. "That long? You kept them that long?"

Lowering her gaze, she rubbed a finger around the edge of the crystal glass. "It was all I had," she said into the cup, not intending him to hear. Forcing herself to smile, Susan looked up. "What's for dinner? I'm starved." She wasn't, but was desperately seeking to change the subject.

"Crepes stuffed with shrimp and fresh mushrooms."

"Adam." Surprise caused her to blink twice. "You can cook like that?"

"Well," he hedged, "not quite, but I do an excellent job of placing something in the oven and setting the timer."

"Oh, Adam," she said happily. "We have so much in common."

They played a game of Monopoly after dinner. Adam won, but Susan's interest wasn't on the board. Adam waited until she'd changed into her pajamas before kissing her good night. The kiss was almost brotherly.

"Miser," she complained.

"Troublemaker," he countered, bringing her back into his arms and kissing her soundly. But he didn't allow it to deepen into passion.

Locking the door after him, Susan leaned against the solid frame and swallowed a happy lump.

Adam was hers.

A half hour later the phone rang and she struggled out of bed, pressing a hand to her ribs as she rose.

"Hello."

"Susan, are you all right?" It was Adam.

"I was until I had to answer the stupid phone," she objected strongly.

"Sorry." His apology was filled with barely contained amusement. "I forgot to tell you not to fix lunch tomorrow."

"Good, why?"

"I'm bringing over something special."

"You mean something more than you."

"That was dumb."

"No dumber than calling me in the middle of the night to talk about lunch."

He chuckled, and Susan was lost in the deep, rich sound of his laughter. "You're right, but I had to hear your voice one more time before I went to bed."

"Oh, Adam." It was one of the most beautiful things he'd ever said to her.

That night was the first of many they spent together as the week progressed. Adam couldn't have been more gentle or loving. He kissed and touched her often. He made excuses to be with her. But he never allowed their lovemaking to rage out of control as it had that first night.

When she was able to return to work, he met her two and sometimes three nights a week. Occasionally they dined out, other times cooking for themselves, or as Adam said, setting the timer. Afterward, she sat at his side reading manuscripts while he looped an arm over her shoulder and worked brainteasers. Susan had never been happier. But late at night, alone, she couldn't push the troubled doubts aside. How much longer would this last before Adam pulled away? Could she bear to let him go?

Three weeks after the accident and it was difficult to tell that anything had happened. Her face had healed beautifully, as Adam repeatedly told her.

Humming happily, she set the table, anticipating Adam's arrival. She placed a candle in the middle of the fresh linen cloth and popped a tuna casserole into the oven. She wasn't much of a cook, but made a humble attempt now and then.

Adam knocked, and when she let him into the apartment, he carelessly tossed his coat over the chair. Surprised at the restrained anger that seemed to exude from him, Susan didn't comment.

She wiped her hands on the apron and kissed him on the cheek. "Have a bad day?"

"No worse than usual."

"I tried my hand at a new recipe and whipped up a tuna casserole."

His razor-sharp gaze sliced into her as he stared at the table. "What's the candle for?"

"No reason," she said, and shrugged. "I thought it might add a little romance to our meal."

"Romance," he spat, viciously throwing the word back at her. "You live and breathe that garbage, don't you?"

Stunned, Susan said nothing for a minute. "If you don't like the candle, then I'll take it away."

"I hate tuna," he shouted at her unreasonably. "I've hated it since I was a kid. If you'd bothered to ask, you might have known that."

"I'm sorry, I . . . I guess I should have."

"Do you have to apologize for every little thing? Don't you ever get tired of groveling?"

Chapter Eight

Susan breathed in sharply in an effort to control her temper. Wordlessly, she walked across the room, took Adam's jacket off the chair and handed it to him.

"It's obvious you've had a rotten day. I'm sorry about that. But I think it would be better for both of us if you left now before you end up wearing the tuna casserole."

"Threats, Susan?" Thick brows arched arrogantly as he issued the question in a calm voice that belied his anger.

Susan wasn't fooled. "We'll have dinner another night." She stalked purposefully across the room and held open the door.

"There won't be another night," he informed her casually. "I should never have let things go this far. The whole situation between us should never have happened. I knew the minute I saw you at Ralph Jordan's that you spelled trouble." He jerked his arm into the jacket. "This is it, Susan."

Did he expect her to cry and beg? She wouldn't, not anymore. If Adam Gallagher could walk out of her life, then she could stand by and let him go. That was the decision she'd made in the hospital and she meant to stick with it.

"Threats, Adam?" She returned his own words.

His shirt was stretched across his broad chest, and Susan directed her gaze to the rippling muscles rather than meet his eyes. Her pulse drummed to an erratic tempo, and she cursed herself for the telltale tremble in her voice.

"Good-bye, Adam," she whispered softly.

He paused as if he wanted to add something, then clamped his mouth tightly shut and stormed out the door.

Gently, Susan closed it, then turned the lock before leaning against the solid wood, needing its support. Her knees felt weak, but with a determined set to her shoulders, she returned to the kitchen, removed one place setting, lit the candle and dished up her dinner.

"My, this is delicious," she spoke out loud. The casserole tasted of overcooked noodles and dried tuna, but she managed to down every bite until her plate was empty.

After washing the dishes she took a long, hot shower and curled up on the sofa to watch television. Her mind was only half on the situation comedy, but she refused to answer the nagging doubts that repeatedly demanded her attention. "No," she whispered forcefully.

"If Adam says we're through then so be it." Hadn't she mentally prepared herself for this? Hadn't she accepted and known from the beginning it would happen? The accident and the closeness they had shared afterward was only a reprieve.

Two miserable days later Susan flew to Florida for the writers' conference. The Boeing 747 took off during a thundering rainstorm and descended from blue skies. This was her first trip to the Sunshine State, and she marveled at the beauty. Although her free time was limited, the conference organizers saw to it that she was given the opportunity to see some of the local sights. Susan only wished her mind had been more on what was happening around her.

She arrived home late Friday afternoon. Absently, she sorted through mail and tossed the bills and junk pieces on the tabletop before carrying her suitcase into the bedroom. Usually home offered a feeling of welcome, peace, a solace that came from things familiar. But not today. She didn't allow her mind to follow its natural course. What was lacking was Adam. Closing her eyes to the hurt, she mentally shook herself. How easily she'd become accustomed to chatting with him, sharing the minor details of her life, that easy camaraderie. Within a space of time he had become her best friend. But admitting the source of the problem did little to lessen the pain of his absence.

Saturday morning, rather than face the day staring at the walls alone, Susan rose early and walked to the office to catch up with the workload that must have reached mountainous proportions on her desk. With her hands stuck deep into her pockets as she strolled, Susan thought how much Rosemary would approve if she could see her now. The walk, although she hated to admit it, was pleasant. Block after block the exercise helped stir her blood and quicken her heartbeat. At least now she felt alive and not half-dead as she had since Adam left.

Letting herself into her small office, the first thing she noticed was a bouquet of flowers. She glanced at them quizzically, unpinning the attached card. It read: "I deserve to wear that casserole. I'm sorry. Meet me at Tastings Thursday. Love, Adam."

Thursday! The flowers must have arrived when she was away. What must he be thinking? Grabbing her coat, she flew out of the office, impatiently tapping her foot on the elevator ride down. Once on the street, she madly waved her arms until she was able to attract the attention of a taxi. The driver steered haphazardly across two lanes of traffic. With a grimace, Susan climbed inside and breathlessly relayed Adam's address.

She almost threw the fare at the astonished man as she leaped from the back seat and raced inside the apartment building. Too impatient for the elevator, she took the stairs, bounding up them two steps at a time until she arrived at the fourth floor and staggered into the hallway.

She was leaning against the wall taking in giant breaths when Adam casually opened the door.

"Adam." Throwing herself into his arms, she hugged him fiercely.

"Susan, are you all right?"

"Yes . . . ," she gasped. "I mean . . . no. Oh, Adam, I was in Florida."

He sat her down on one of the two wing-backed chairs that dominated his living room and left her for a moment while he went into the kitchen.

If her legs hadn't felt like cooked noodles, she would have gone after him. "Adam," she pleaded.

"Here." He handed her a glass of water and knelt in front of her.

She set the water aside, and with eyes sparkling with happiness, she placed her hands on his shoulders. "I've missed you so much." Closing her eyes, she leaned forward until their foreheads touched. Lovingly her hands traced his jaw.

His fingers stopped hers and brought them to his lips. "You idiot," he groaned, and hugged her. "There was no need to half kill yourself to get to me. I already knew you were in Florida. When you didn't show, I called your office and asked—"

"You called?" she asked incredulously.

"What's so unusual about that? I call you all the time."

"I know, but never after a fight. Never!"

"We don't argue," he contradicted, a crooked smile tugging up the edges of his mouth.

"Adam, for heaven's sake, would you stop being so obtuse! I can't stand it."

Her happy gaze met his as he kissed her hungrily. Every minute of their separation, each second apart, was worth the thrill of Adam's touch.

"Were you miserable?" she asked him.

"Yes," he replied on a forceful note.

"I love it," she cried cheerfully, but her heart repeated that it was Adam she really loved. "But if you were so down and out, why didn't you meet me at the airport?"

"I was planning on it. You weren't due in until this afternoon."

"That's right,"she murmured, more pleased than she could remember being about anything. "I was able to connect with a flight yesterday afternoon and opted to come home early," she whispered in a rush, and threw her arms around him a second time. "Oh, Adam." She swallowed the lump of joy that blocked her throat. "I'm so pleased to be home."

He took her to the Palm Court at the Plaza Hotel, and they lunched on luscious salads. Not until the meal was finished did Susan notice the pinched look about Adam's mouth.

"I've been talking fifty miles an hour and hardly giving you time to say a word."

Adam swirled the wineglass, and the imported Soave sloshed over the edge. "What do you want me to say?" The smile didn't reach his eyes.

"I could think of several wonderful lines," she whispered. Like "I love you, Susan Mackenzie," her mind added.

"I'm sure you can." His eyes avoided hers.

Sighing softly, she reached across the table for his hand. "Adam, what's wrong?"

Wearily he rubbed his face. "It's been one of those weeks. I've been miserable without you, Susan."

He needed her, but he wouldn't admit as much.

Something deep and dark was troubling him. He couldn't hide it from her; she knew him too well. Perhaps that bothered him more.

"Didn't you say something about picking up some work at your office?"

Susan nodded. "Do you want to meet me back at my place later? I'll cook us dinner." Looking at the leftover food on her plate, she added, "Something light."

"Fine." He took his wallet from inside his coat. "I've got a few errands to do. I'll see you tonight."

As it turned out it was much later. When Adam hadn't shown up by eight, she frowned and dialed his number. The phone rang ten times before she replaced the receiver. Perplexed, she sat on the sofa, feet crossed, as she read over book proposals she'd brought home from the office. Nothing held her concentration as her gaze swung to her watch every five minutes. Where was Adam?

When the doorbell chimed she nearly leaped off the couch. "Hi," she said, and didn't mention how late he was or ask why.

Again his smile didn't reach his eyes. "Sorry, I didn't mean to take this long." He didn't offer any information or excuses.

"No problem. I wasn't hungry. Do you want me to fix you something?"

"Sure," he agreed.

Susan suspected he only wanted dinner so she'd be kept busy in the kitchen and wouldn't ask questions. When he barely touched the scrambled eggs and bacon, she knew she was right.

He wrapped his arms around her later when they sat on the sofa. Again she noted the sadness in his eyes as he laid his head against the back cushion.

"Adam?" she questioned softly. "What's wrong?"

"Nothing," he denied a second time. He closed his eyes and released a deep sigh. Susan watched him, all the more troubled.

"Let me massage your temples. You look like you've got a headache." Standing behind him, she gently pressed her fingertips in a rotating movement against the sides of his head. Gradually she worked her way down his neck to his shoulders. The muscles were tense and corded as if every inch of him were prepared to spring into action.

"That feels good." His head began to move in a circular action, keeping rhythm with her hands. "Want me to do you?"

"No," she answered, and gently laid her lips along the side of his neck. "Mmmm, you smell good. What is that?"

He chuckled, the first time she'd heard his laugh since that morning. "Antiseptic."

"It isn't either," she insisted, and gave a shout of surprise as he tumbled her over the back of the sofa into his arms and kissed her long and hard. In the past his kisses had been deep, but now there was a punishing quality to the way his mouth ground over hers. Weakly she submitted, knowing he needed her and was using her. She gave him what she could.

When he released her, Adam's gaze narrowed briefly at her swollen lips. "Did I hurt you?"

"No," she lied in an attempt to assure him she didn't mind.

His thumb traced her throbbing mouth in a gentle, soothing movement. "Did I mention that Joey Williams was back in the hospital?" He said it so casually that for a moment she didn't recognize the significance.

"No." She breathed in deeply. "No you didn't." So that was it. Joey. The little boy Adam loved. "How . . . how's he doing?"

Adam didn't respond immediately. Instead he picked up one of her manuscripts and leafed through the neatly typed pages. She knew what he was thinking as clearly as if he had shouted the words. The books she edited were filled with the light side of life, fantasy, happy-ever-after. But not for Joey. And not in the world in which Adam lived and worked.

"Not good," Adam answered at last. "What happens when someone submits a manuscript?" He was purposely changing the subject. He gathered her in his arms, holding her head against his chest.

She spoke because she knew that was what he wanted. "Did you know Silhouette receives seven hundred manuscripts a month, far more than a handful of editors can deal with?"

"Seven hundred," he repeated. "I knew these books were popular, if my mother is anything to go by, but seven hundred hopefuls every month? My goodness!"

Susan smiled softly. "If someone submits a full manuscript instead of a proposal—"

"What's a proposal?"

"Three chapters and an outline."

She felt his nod against the top of her head. The slow drum of his heart sounded reassuring in her ear.

"What happens then?"

"A full manuscript goes to a freelance reader, who reads the book and writes a report on it before an editor looks it over."

"What about the proposals?"

"The editors divide the work load and get to them as quickly as possible."

"That's what you're reading now?"

She nodded. "I enjoy it. Some of our best writers were discovered in the slush pile."

"Where does an agent play into this?"

Susan laughed lightly. "You'll have to ask Ralph that one. He does a good job of sticking material under my nose whenever he gets the chance."

"Okay, suppose you want to buy someone's book."

"It's called acquiring. Then I either talk to that person's agent or directly to them. We agree on an advance and I send the order through to the managing editor in the contracts department. That's where Rosemary works, by the way."

A hand smoothed a curl away from her neck as his fingers toyed with her hair. Susan was sure he was only half listening.

"After the author signs and returns the contract, some of the advance is issued. I put through another payment request for the second half when the manuscript is completed and any revisions needed are done. Then the book is scheduled. With twenty-eight books released each month, this is more difficult than most people realize. For instance, we don't want five books coming out all located in Kansas City. And titles can be a hassle.''

''I bet they are,'' he mumbled.

''Adam,'' she admonished gently, ''you haven't heard a word I said.''

''Sure I did.''

Rather than argue, Susan straightened. ''Want to play cribbage?'' They had played the card game several times in the past. Their skill was equally matched, but when she won three games running, she realized Adam's mind wasn't in it.

Adam helped her pick up the board and cards. ''Walk me to the door,'' he requested lightly.

Susan did as he asked, then slipped her arms around his neck, anticipating his kiss. Slowly his eyes lowered to look into hers. His troubled features mirrored all the turbulent emotions he had stored inside his heart.

The hand at the back of her neck tightened, urging her mouth to his. Susan's lips parted in eager welcome as his mouth consumed hers.

''Adam.'' She released his name on a rush of air. Desperately she longed to share his burden. Compulsively she molded her body to his, as if to bring him as close as physically possible. Was there anything so insurmountable that they couldn't face and conquer it together? ''I'll see you . . .''

''You'll see me.'' He released her and kissed her forehead. ''I don't know when.''

''It's okay. I understand.''

His brilliant dark eyes narrowed. ''Do you, Susan?''

''Yes.'' She nodded, emphasizing that she did.

"I don't want to hurt you again. I hate myself afterward."

"You aren't going to hurt me," she countered softly. "I'm a big girl."

He kissed her again lightly before letting himself out.

Susan didn't hear from him until Tuesday of the following week. He phoned late one night.

"Hi, honey, how's your week going?"

"Fine, and you?"

"Great." The word was emitted in a flippant tone, and Susan wanted to shout at him that it wasn't necessary for him to lie to her.

"Any news?" She didn't need to clarify about whom.

"Nothing," he responded in the same tone. "What about you?"

"One of the editors is sick and it looks like I'll be traveling to Texas soon."

"Another conference? Do you usually travel this much?"

"We all do our share, but it usually isn't more than a couple of times a year." Was Adam suggesting that he didn't want her to go, that he may need her? She broached the subject carefully. "Is there a problem? I mean, I'm sure one of the other editors wouldn't mind."

"It's no problem for me," Adam returned. "Why should I care?"

Indeed! Susan bristled. They spoke for a few minutes longer, but the conversation was unsatisfactory and left Susan deflated and angry.

They met for dinner early the next week. Susan was

several minutes late and found Adam already seated and studying the menu when she arrived.

"Sorry, but I got held up in traffic," she said in a slightly breathless tone as she slid into the seat opposite him and shrugged off her coat.

Adam looked up, but only said, "Are you ready to order?"

"Order?" she asked. "I've barely caught my breath. Adam, you wouldn't believe the day I've had. First I got stuck on the phone with an agent who was making the most unreasonable demands. And just before I left an author called wanting to go over the editorial changes I'd made on her manuscript. Over the phone, mind you. It just seemed to be one thing right after the other."

He offered her a poor facsimile of a smile.

"I'm sorry, Adam," she said sincerely. "I didn't even ask about your day."

"Nothing unusual. Mine certainly can't compete with a popular romance editor's day."

Susan decided to ignore the sarcastic tone. "Ralph Jordan called today. He's giving another party. Are we going?"

"We?" He raised one thick brow.

Deliberately, Susan laid the menu beside her plate. "Adam, what is wrong with you? You haven't said a civil word since I arrived."

"Not for lack of trying, I assure you." His face was buried in the menu, blocking her out. "With you chattering away with inanities, it's difficult to speak at all."

Susan expelled a slow, measured breath, trying with

great difficulty to maintain her limited patience. "Is it Joey?"

He slammed the menu on the table, the commotion attracting the attention of others. "Joey's home; are you satisfied?" He was nearly shouting, his voice biting and bitter.

Unbelievably hurt, Susan closed her eyes to a rush of pain. She never would have believed Adam could talk to her that way.

"Don't tell me you're going to cry. I can't stand women who cry."

For a long minute Susan said nothing. "I used to think you were the gentlest man I'd ever known. Something's wrong, Adam. It's obvious you don't want to share it with me, and that's your prerogative. But something's got to be done. Over the last couple of weeks I find it difficult to even like you."

"Maybe that's the way I want it."

"Then why invite me to dinner? Why phone me? Certainly you're not enjoying this any more than I am?"

His eyes were sad and haunted. "For the first time all night, you're talking sense. Why are we here? What the hell do we have in common? You're the beautiful romance editor who lives in never-never land among the happily-ever-afters."

"I think I've heard enough." Scooting out of the booth, she stood beside him and hurriedly placed her arms inside her coat sleeves. "When you've settled whatever's troubling you, then give me a call. I'll be waiting."

He started to say something, but Susan didn't wait to

listen. Instead she hurried out of the restaurant and hailed a taxi before he had the opportunity to follow.

Another week passed before she heard from Adam again. He called to apologize, but he didn't suggest they meet and she didn't ask.

Ralph Jordan's dinner party came and went. She didn't attend and assumed Adam hadn't either.

Susan couldn't recall a more frustrating time. Adam was not the same man she'd met. Examining the two sides of his personality was like seeing two entirely different people. She felt helpless and lost, cold and empty. Even Rosemary noticed things weren't right.

"You don't look good. I don't think you're getting enough vitamin A."

"Honestly, Rosemary, I'm fine."

"I'm serious," her friend returned. "Vitamin A as in Adam."

Susan grinned. "No, I suppose I'm not. I haven't seen him in almost two weeks, one day and"—she lifted her arm to examine her wristwatch—"eighteen hours. Not that I care."

"I noticed," her friend murmured. "You know what the problem is, don't you?"

Interested now, Susan had a difficult time containing a smile. "No, tell me."

"You know one another too well."

Susan gave a good-natured laugh. Some days she didn't think she knew Adam at all. Certainly not these last weeks.

"Fred and I knew in one day . . ."

"How'd you know?" Susan asked seriously, the amusement slowly dissipating.

"Well we'd gone out to dinner and the fortune cookie said—"

"You mean to tell me," Susan interrupted, "that you and Fred got married on the sound advice of a fortune cookie? Rosemary Thomas Bradly, I am shocked."

Rosemary had the good grace to blush. "You mean because we were married so soon?"

"No, silly," Susan said, "that's romantic. I'm shocked that the two of you were eating Chinese food with all the MSG and heart-bending toxicants."

Later, when Susan lay in bed staring at the ceiling, it wasn't as easy to put on a smile and tease. There were only the darkness and the doubts. How could a man who was gentle and kind one minute turn into a snarling, unreasonable bear the next? Maybe she was totally wrong about him. Maybe the time had come for her to . . .

The doorbell interrupted her thoughts.

Susan sat up and threw back her bedcovers. A quick look at the clock assured her it was well past midnight. Who could it possibly be at this time of night? After tying the sash to her robe, she turned on the light switch in the living room.

The bell sounded again.

Peeking out the small hole in her door, Susan saw no one. "Who is it?" she called.

For a moment there was nothing.

"Adam."

Chapter Nine

"Adam," Susan said softly as she unlocked the door.

He hesitated, searching her face as if desperate for the sight of her. "I woke you."

"No," she told him. "I'd gone to bed, but I wasn't asleep. Come in."

"I don't think . . ." He paused and looked past her into the dimly lit room. "A cup of coffee would help."

"I'll put some on right away." Her eyes didn't leave him as he came into the apartment and slowly lowered himself onto the sofa. He looked terrible. Susan couldn't remember seeing anyone so pale.

Moving quickly, she poured water into the tea kettle. As she worked, Susan glanced into the room at Adam. He was leaning forward, elbows on his knees with his face buried in his palms. For the first time she noticed the bloody knuckles on one hand. Adam had been fighting? She couldn't believe it.

He must have felt her scrutiny because he dropped his arms and sat up. Never had Susan seen a look more filled with pain. A torment so deep it reached all the way to his soul.

After setting the kettle on the stove, she moved to his side, kneeling in front of him. "Adam," she whispered, all the love in her heart shining through her eyes. "What is it? Won't you tell me?"

Although he looked directly at her, Susan was sure he was hardly aware she was there. "Joey Williams died tonight."

A soft protesting moan came from deep within her throat. "Oh, Adam," she whispered, her voice shaking, "I'm so sorry." Sliding her arms around his stomach, she rested her face on his chest and started to cry. "You loved him so much." Sobs shook her.

Adam resisted and tried to push her away, but she wouldn't let him, tightening her grip around this man she loved. He held himself stiff and unyielding until something seemed to snap within him.

He shuddered against her and released a deep, mournful cry like that of an animal caught in a trap, facing death. Fiercely he hauled her into his arms, hugging her so close that for a moment Susan was afraid he would crush her. Hugh sobs wracked his body as he buried his face in her neck and wept.

"His mother wanted him to die at home," Adam told her with a sobbing breath. "I knew he wouldn't last much longer, and tonight she had me lift him into her arms. He died there two hours ago."

"Adam," Susan cried, wanting so badly to comfort him.

"All the years I studied and there wasn't a damn thing I could do. Never have I felt so damn helpless."

"You did everything you could," she whispered soothingly.

"Not enough, not near enough."

She couldn't understand anything more he said, his words muffled in her hair and by his tears. She didn't know how long he held her. As the shuddering sobs subsided, she heard the brittle whistle from the kettle on the stove.

Briefly Adam raised his head, noting the source of the distraction. Reluctantly he released her.

Before she left, Susan lifted his hand and kissed his bloody knuckles. She walked to the kitchen and wiped her face dry, then poured them each a steaming cup and returned to Adam.

His eyes remained red and haunted, and his gaze avoided hers as he took the coffee. "Thank you," he murmured.

Susan knew he wasn't referring to the drink.

Neither spoke. They didn't need words. The closeness between them was beyond expression.

After a few sips of steaming liquid, Susan placed her cup aside. Adam curved an arm around her shoulder, bringing her close. She rested against him while his hand tenderly stroked the length of her arm.

When the soothing action stopped, Susan lifted her head and noticed that Adam was asleep.

Carefully, so not to wake him, she slipped from his embrace. He was exhausted, mentally and physically.

When his head dropped to one side, she brought out a pillow and blanket from her bedroom. With only a minimum of encouragement she was able to ease his head onto the feathery softness. After removing his shoes, she lifted his feet onto the sofa and covered him with a blanket.

Even in sleep, his look remained troubled. Susan stood and watched him for a long time. He had come to her in his grief, and that meant more to her than the finest gifts. Because what he had given her, his trust and love, was beyond price.

Flipping the switch to the lamp cast the room into darkness. Susan paused, standing above Adam. Gently she bent down, lovingly brushed the thick hair from his forehead and kissed him.

When she woke the next morning Adam was gone. A scribbled note left on the kitchen table briefly thanked her and stated the date and time of the funeral. With her morning coffee cupped in her hands, Susan fingered the plain piece of paper. Joey's death explained so much of Adam's behavior these past weeks. Why hadn't he said something? She expelled a frustrated sigh when she recalled that he'd tried the day he told her Joey was back in the hospital. Perhaps she should have pressed him more. But at the time she didn't feel she could. Adam had known then that there was nothing he could do for the child and had carried the burden all these weeks.

She remembered the day she'd met Joey, the twinkling, happy eyes and the love and admiration the boy had for Adam. Later when she'd asked Adam if Joey

was going to make it, Adam had answered her with an
emphatic yes as if he had infused his own fierce
determination into the child, lending the boy a part of
himself. With Joey's death, that part of Adam had died.

Susan didn't see Adam until the day of the funeral.
She slipped into the pew beside him and listened to the
comforting words of the beautiful service. Her hand
was tightly clenched in his.

Afterward the Williams family came over to Adam.
Mrs. Williams, tears glistening in her proud eyes,
hugged him.

"We owe you more than words can ever express,"
she said. "Thank you for making it possible for Joey to
come home those last days."

Mr. Williams, pale and drawn, shook Adam's hand,
and Mrs. Williams smiled weakly at Susan.

"You must be Miss Mackenzie. Joey mentioned how
pretty you are." She inclined her head toward Adam.
"Hold on to this man," she whispered. "There aren't
many as wonderful as Dr. Gallagher."

"I know that," Susan agreed.

"In the end he hardly left Joey's side. The Lord
knows when he slept. Our family will never forget
him."

Susan nodded because the lump in her throat had
grown so large it was impossible to speak.

"Honestly, Rosemary, I don't know how I let you
talk me into these things," Susan complained under her
breath as she moved her body in rhythm to the
fast-paced music that filled the gym.

"You love it and you know it," Rosemary returned, only slightly breathless.

"Well darn it, if we're going to do this aerobics thing, the least you can do is sweat. I'm wringing wet."

"If you were in better—"

"Don't say it," Susan warned. "Besides, pregnant women aren't supposed to be able to do this kind of thing."

"Jane Fonda does."

It was becoming increasingly difficult to talk, and Susan wondered what Jane Fonda had to do with this. Her feelings toward the talented actress were decidedly unpleasant at the moment. Weakly, Susan motioned with her hand that she'd had enough. Panting, she leaned against the wall of the gymnasium, waiting until Rosemary had finished the routine. Rosemary leaped enthusiastically with each beat of the music. The only evidence that her friend was pregnant was the gentle swell of Rosemary's abdomen. Susan watched her, longing for the day she could have a child. Adam's child. Already she knew a boy would be named Joey, although she'd never discussed it with Adam.

Within a few minutes Rosemary joined Susan. "You were smart to stop when you did since this is your first session."

"My body knows when it's had enough."

"There's a word for that," Rosemary murmured, pinching her bottom lip with two fingers as she thought.

"It's called wisdom."

Rosemary poked her with an elbow. "Know-it-all! Come on, let's go have some carrot juice."

Susan shook her head. "No thanks, I brought my own drink."

"Diet soda?" Rosemary asked in a whisper.

Susan nodded.

"Well for heaven's sake, don't let anyone around here see you drinking it. You'll be railroaded out of the place."

"I'll have the carrot juice," she grumbled.

Round white enameled tables were set in a sun room with a refreshment bar. Susan located a vacant table while Rosemary brought back their drinks. The place was packed. Susan couldn't understand how so many women could torture themselves this way for thinner thighs. As far as she was concerned, it was all genetic anyway.

One sip of the orange-colored juice and Susan grimaced.

Rosemary laughed softly. "I had them spice it up a little."

"With what?" Susan demanded, then abruptly shook her hand. "Never mind, I don't want to know."

Dark expressive eyes sparkled cheerfully as Rosemary took another sip from the straw. "It's probably best you don't."

"That did it." Hurriedly Susan pushed the drink aside.

"I was teasing. It's just carrot juice."

"Sure," Susan murmured, and bent down to pull up her leg warmers, which had slipped ingloriously around her ankles.

"Have you seen much of Adam lately?" Apparently Rosemary had thought it best to change the subject.

"Quite regularly."

"Honestly, you two should get married. What are you waiting for?"

"A proposal."

"Well, that's silly, you—"

"It's not silly at all. If we're going to get married, I think it's only right that Adam do the asking. I was the one who asked him out the first time. And he refused; that still rankles."

"Has he said he loves you?" Rosemary looked worried.

"A thousand times," Susan confirmed, and sighed heavily. "But never with words."

"Perhaps he needs a little prompting?"

"Not from me," she stated emphatically. "For once I'm going to keep my mouth shut."

Taking a sip of her drink, Rosemary mumbled, "For you, that must be difficult."

"Have you got everything?" Adam questioned as he lifted her suitcase.

"I think so." Susan did a quick survey of her bedroom. Everything looked neatly in place. The items she needed were carefully packed in her suitcases.

"I'm ready." Adam was driving her to the airport. After dinner she would be flying to Boston for a promotional tour with several authors. The tour would be five days of interviews, talks and traveling. Susan always enjoyed working with the publicity department. But now she almost regretted having agreed to go. Something was happening with Adam, but she had no idea what.

"That look is in your eyes again," she told him as they sat in the cozy restaurant not far from the airport.

"What look?" He glanced up, his fingers busy, gently twirling the wineglass.

"The one in your eyes," she repeated. "Since we've arrived, you've toyed with your napkin, fiddled with your fork, and done everything possible not to look at me."

"That's because every time I stare into those gorgeous eyes of yours I'm tempted to toss good manners out the window and pull you into my arms."

"That sounds interesting," she teased, but Adam ignored her, pretending he hadn't heard. Susan knew differently.

Even his kisses had been different lately, almost polite yet wonderful and gentle. She didn't know how to explain it. But now wasn't the time to discuss it.

When it came time to board her flight, Susan couldn't fault his kiss then. He found a quiet corner that offered as much privacy as possible and unhurriedly drew her into his embrace. Susan studied the strong, uneven lines of his face. Adam Gallagher was a vital, compelling man although he insisted he was "plain looking." Even if it was true, Susan was no longer aware of that aspect of Adam. She saw the man, as she had that first night when she'd only guessed at the vibrancy within him that made her heart sing.

"I'm going to miss you." His voice was a caress, husky and warm.

"Good, because you know how I feel." Adam had never verbalized the words, but neither had she. A thousand times she was forced to swallow back the natural flow of her love. From the first time they'd met, it had always been her. Adam's mother had told her to be patient, and for now she would be content, although it grew more difficult as each week passed. He loved her. She knew it without the words. When he told her, it would be from his heart and so much more meaningful than if she prompted him.

"Yes, I do."

She heard the taut pain in his voice and narrowed her gaze, perplexed.

"Yes, I do," he repeated, as he lowered his mouth to savor the softness of hers. The kiss was slow and exploring, his tongue outlining her lips, coaxing her mouth open. Gladly Susan succumbed to the sweet tide of longing that swept through her.

Time away from New York helped put her relationship with Adam into perspective, but it didn't offer the answer to the doubts that plagued her. Several times she toyed with the idea of phoning with one excuse or another, knowing she only needed to hear his voice. Usually late at night when she knew he'd be asleep. Or early in the morning when he'd be busy. As much as she hated to admit it, calling him probably wasn't the best thing.

When the plane touched down at Kennedy, she eagerly anticipated their meeting.

He waved when he saw her, and Susan had to restrain herself from running into his arms. Adam looked wonderful. The color was back in his face; his eyes were warm and excited. It'd been so long since she'd seen him this happy.

"Welcome home." He looped an arm around her waist, took her hand baggage and kissed her cheek.

"You look marvelous."

"I am. How was the trip?"

"Great," she said, and sighed. "But I must admit it's good to be home."

He squeezed her close. "It's good to have you back. I've got some fantastic news."

"What?" She stopped walking so she could watch him.

"I've accepted a position in Seattle, Washington, at the Fred Hutchinson Cancer Research Center. I'm moving next week."

Chapter Ten

"Seattle, Washington?" The words went through her like a bolt of lightning and she paused, stunned, as the shock hit her full force.

"It's the opportunity of a lifetime," Adam continued, undaunted by her obvious surprise. "I can't tell you how pleased and excited I am."

He didn't need to tell her; it was there for her to see. "Congratulations," she murmured, a breathless quiver to her voice.

"Honey, I think you'll understand that I've got a hundred and one things that need to be done. Meeting you tonight was important and I did want to tell you my good news. But I've got to get back to my office right away. You understand, don't you?"

"Oh, sure. Of course I do." Fixing a smile on her face, she wondered if he detected the forced quality in her voice. Numbly she followed him to the baggage claim area, barely aware of where they were going.

When he carried her suitcases into the apartment, she stepped aside, a determined lift to her chin. He kissed her at the door. A brotherly kiss.

"Be happy for me." His voice vibrated with the depth of his feeling.

"I'm thrilled," she lied. *I'm dying,* her heart answered.

He hesitated, his gaze playing over her profile.

"I appreciate that you came to the airport, but it really wasn't necessary." A weary sigh escaped and she looked away.

"I wanted to, Susan." He glanced at his wristwatch.

"Go," she commanded, fighting to keep the sarcasm out of her voice. "I understand."

She understood all too well. Adam was running. Running from New York, running from the memories of the little boy he couldn't save. But most of all he was running from her love. Her suitcases were just inside the door, and Susan looked around with a feeling of desolation. Within days she would be losing Adam, the most important person in her life. A heavy weight settled over her heart.

She barely slept. Just when she felt herself drifting off, the pain would return and she'd jerk awake.

Because she couldn't tolerate the thought of staying in the apartment on a Saturday morning, she dressed and walked to the park. Hands buried deep in her pockets, Susan sauntered around the soccer field. The season was over and the chalk line that bordered the playing area had faded long ago. But the happy thoughts the area evoked were fresh and potent.

"Are you going to let him do this?" her voice asked. *Yes,* her heart answered, knowing there was nothing she could do to stop him.

Hating herself for being weak, she phoned him when she got back to the apartment.

"Hello." He sounded preoccupied, busy.

"Morning," she said on a falsely cheerful note. "Have you had breakfast?"

"No time, I'm sorting through my things, deciding what I want to take and what I'm going to store at my mother's. It's shocking how much stuff I've accumulated in the last few years."

"Let me help you. I'll stop by the bakery on my way over and bring some croissants."

The pause was only momentary. "Sure."

"I'll stay afterward and help you pack books and stuff."

"There's no need," Adam answered unevenly.

I'm not letting you go that easily, her mind shouted. "I want to help."

"If you like." He didn't sound as if *he* did.

"I want to," she repeated.

The flaky croissants were still warm from the oven, but neither Susan nor Adam seemed to have much appetite. Carrying the paper plates into the kitchen, she dumped the leftovers in the garbage. With a shaky smile, she pushed up the sleeves of her sweatshirt.

"I'm ready. Where would you like me to start?"

Boxes littered the living room. Most of the furniture

was pushed to one side of the room. Bookcases filled
with leather-bound books stood against one wall.

"Go ahead and pack up those."

He left her alone, and went to work in his den. Susan
recognized that the move was intentional. He didn't
want to be with her, was avoiding her as much as
possible.

Lovingly she ran her hand over a worn copy of *The
Citadel* by A. J. Cronin. In some ways Adam was like
this frustrated, unhappy doctor.

As she carefully placed the books inside the boxes,
she examined each one with the knowledge that she
was learning more and more about Adam. From the
things he treasured, he gave away a part of himself.

Susan could hear his movements in the other room.
After a half hour of silence she called to him.

"Do you want a cup of coffee?"

"Sounds great. I could do with a break."

She poured them each a cup and sat on the plush
carpet drinking hers. Adam didn't seem to want to stop
working and continued going through his desk drawers.

"There's a chance I'll be in Seattle sometime in
June." She didn't add that was when her vacation was
scheduled. Purposely she let him think it was business
related.

"Wonderful." He didn't sound as if he meant it.

"My parents live in Oregon."

He stopped what he was doing and looked up. "I'd
forgotten that."

Of course he had. Washington State was as far away
from her as he could get, and without knowing it he'd

placed himself in her home territory. She watched as a frown worked its way across his face.

"But I think I should warn you, my schedule is very tight," he explained.

Susan didn't know how much more of this she could take. He was saying that if she did come, he'd make excuses not to see her. Cradling her knees, she stared into the dark coffee. Usually she drank it thick and dark. Today she added several teaspoons of sugar, knowing she needed energy. Rosemary would have been aghast. A sad smile touched her face.

"What's so funny?" Adam asked.

"My thoughts, I guess."

The natural question would have been to ask her what she was thinking, but Adam didn't. Perhaps he was afraid of what she'd say.

"I'll finish packing the books," she said, and stood.

"Susan." Her name was issued on a soft, anguish-filled tone.

She turned around. "Yes?" Her eyes pleaded with him, but he shook his head and looked away. "Your desk must be piled high. I've never known you not to go to the office on a Saturday after a business trip."

"There's nothing pressing," she told him casually. No, she wasn't going to make this easy for him. Not one bit. He was going to have to shove her away. It didn't matter if he pushed her so hard that she stumbled and fell backward. Because somehow, some way, she would pick herself up again. She was a survivor, if nothing else.

Two boxes were already filled and Susan scooted

them aside. She pulled a third cardboard case across the carpet, then carefully slid out the bottom row of books. As she did, several Christmas cards fell onto the floor. One was a flowery, romantic one that immediately attracted her attention with its huge red poinsettia and the bold words calligraphed across the top: "TO THE WOMAN I LOVE." Another was a humorous one, identical to one that Susan had read that Christmas while looking for a special card for Adam.

Sharply she sucked in her breath. Four cards had spilled onto the carpet, each one fresh and unsigned. Adam had bought these cards for her. He'd deny it vehemently if she were fool enough to confront him. But she knew. Because she had done the same thing.

Acid tears stung the back of her eyes, burning for release.

"Susan, would you mind . . ." Adam came into the room and paused when he found her posed with the cards in her hands. "Throw that stuff away. They're just some old cards that must have fallen back there from Christmas."

"They're unsigned." One tear weaved a path down her face.

"Yes, well, just throw them away."

Another tear joined the first, followed by several more. "I don't understand you, Adam Gallagher."

He rammed a hand along the side of his head. "Damn it. I knew this was going to happen. You know how I feel about tears."

With all the frustration and anger burning inside, Susan hurled the cards at him. "You have no idea, do you?"

"Idea?" He stared at her blankly.

"I ate tofu on a cracker for you," she shouted, nearly choking on her tears. "I practically killed myself just for the pleasure of running with you. I could barely make it over speed bumps and I was cheerfully jogging miles and miles just to be near you."

"Susan, stop it," he demanded. "You're not making any sense."

"I'm making perfect sense," she shouted unreasonably, waving her arms.

"Susan, please."

"I swallowed my pride so many times I nearly gagged on it." Sobbing uncontrollably, she stormed from one room to another, finally locating some tissues with which to blow her nose.

Stunned, Adam stood in the hallway looking dumbfounded.

"You know what your problem is?" She pointed a finger at him. "You don't need to answer that because I'm going to tell you. Adam Gallagher, you're a coward." She noticed a muscle move against the side of his jaw, but it didn't stop her. Bending down, she picked up the card with the poinsettia. "Just who were you intending to give this to? Your mother?"

"No." He glared at her. "Gail."

The anger drained out of her as she stared back at him speechlessly. Somehow she never believed he'd resort to lying.

"Okay, Adam." Her voice caught on a sob. "You won't say it, so I will. I love you. I'll love you all my life. Move to Washington! Have a good life! But I swear I'm going to haunt you. When you look into another woman's eyes it'll be my face you'll see. When you run in the mornings it'll be my footsteps you'll hear behind you. And . . . when you look into some little boy's face, you'll see the son you wouldn't give me." Tears were streaming uncontrollably down her cheeks now. Wiping them aside, she looked at him one last time. He stood proud, defensive, stubborn . . . and insecure. "Good-bye, Adam." The words were issued softly, belying the inner turmoil. Taking her jacket, she stepped out of his apartment and out of his life.

She walked when she wanted to run, swallowed back the sobs when her heart was breaking. By the time she was on the street, the tears had abated and the weight in her heart seemed to press harder and heavier.

Before she was aware of her destination, Susan found herself in Central Park. Her eyes were dry now, but she sniffled as she strolled along the footpath. For old times, she told herself.

She paused at the bench where they'd met in the mornings, and ran a hand longingly over the painted wood surface. Those few short days were the happiest of her life. Dejected and miserable, she sat, leaned against the back of the bench, stretched out her legs and crossed them at the ankles. Her chin was buried in her jacket.

She'd done it again—made a fool of herself in front of Adam. Fool or no fool, how could he leave her when she loved him so much?

Someone sat at the other end of the bench. Susan took it to be a stranger until he assumed the same position as she, crossing his feet at the ankles. Those shoes were lovingly familiar. Adam's shoes. He didn't say a word. She didn't either. Forcing herself to stare directly ahead of her, she didn't move, hardly breathed.

"I have to go away," he said in a controlled voice that seemed devoid of emotion.

Susan said nothing.

"I'm so much in love with you that I can't hide it anymore."

She didn't move, the words paralyzing her.

"When we first met I couldn't believe someone as beautiful as you could be interested in a nobody like me."

The argument was old. She was sick of it and refused to be drawn into it again.

"Later, when I learned you were a romance editor," he continued, "I knew it would never work. But I already loved you, and as much as I tried to force myself to leave you alone, sever our relationship, I couldn't."

"Why?" The one word came out high and uneven.

"Because I can never be like the men in those books. The man every woman dreams about, the kind of man you deserve. I'm not rich, dark, or handsome. I'm a weak man. The night Joey died, I proved to you just how weak I am. A man crying. That must be a first for you. I'll never be the strong and silent type."

"What makes you think I want that?" Still she didn't turn or look at him.

"It would be impossible for you to read and not compare me with the hero in those books. Maybe not at first, but eventually; and when the comparison came, I'd fall short. With Gail I made the mistake of believing a woman could love me in spite of my plainness. I don't want to make that mistake again."

"Don't compare me to Gail," she hissed.

"It's not only that," he murmured. "You work with beautiful people and unreal situations. I deal with reality."

"I love you, Adam," she told him, hands clenched in her pockets. "You, Dr. Adam Gallagher, not some insensitive, conceited male whose interests revolve around himself. I'm flesh and blood and capable of distinguishing between fantasy and reality."

"You were right when you said I'm a coward. I'm more of one than you know. I was in the park watching you last Christmas. Hiding."

"Hiding? When?" For the first time she turned her head to look at him. He was pale, his mouth tight, the eyes dark but brilliant.

"I called you and purposely mentioned something about running, hoping you'd come to the park. Yet when you did, I stood in the distance, unable to come to you. Afraid that when I saw you again, I wouldn't be able to hide my love."

She released a shuddering breath. "You know, Adam, I was the one who introduced myself to you. I asked you to kiss me that first time. I followed you, made excuses to see you. Nearly killed myself to become physically fit to run with you. Made an utter fool of myself so many times I've lost count. I even had to be the one to tell you I was in love first. But so help me, if I end up proposing, I'll never forgive you."

"Will this help?" He took something out of his

pocket, flipped open the velvet top and handed it to her.

Susan sat up shocked. A diamond engagement ring from Tiffanys. Her mouth dropped open, but words refused to come. "When? How?"

"I got the ring after the accident. I knew then I couldn't live without you."

"Why has it taken you so long?" she asked in a painful gasp.

Adam took the ring from the case and slipped it on her finger. A smile of immense pleasure turned up the edges of his mouth. "I was just waiting for the right moment."

"Oh, Adam!" She smiled and threw herself into his arms.